FREE WILLY 2

THE ADVENTURE HOME

FREE WILLY 2

THE ADVENTURE HOME

A novelization by Jordan Horowitz
Based on the Motion Picture
Written by Karen Janszen and Corey Blechman and John Mattson
Based on Characters Created by Keith A. Walker

SCHOLASTIC INC.
New York Toronto London Auckland Sydney

FREE WILLY 2
THE ADVENTURE HOME

WARNER BROS. PRESENTS

IN ASSOCIATION WITH LE STUDIO CANAL+, REGENCY ENTERPRISES AND ALCOR FILMS   A SHULER-DONNER / DONNER PRODUCTION   A DWIGHT LITTLE FILM   JASON JAMES RICHTER   "FREE WILLY 2: THE ADVENTURE HOME"

AUGUST SCHELLENBERG   JAYNE ATKINSON   JON TENNEY   ELIZABETH PEÑA AND MICHAEL MADSEN   MUSIC BY BASIL POLEDOURIS   CO-PRODUCER RICHARD SOLOMON

EXECUTIVE PRODUCERS RICHARD DONNER, ARNON MILCHAN, JIM VAN WYCK   WRITTEN BY KAREN JANSZEN AND COREY BLECHMAN AND JOHN MATTSON

PRODUCED BY LAUREN SHULER-DONNER AND JENNIE LEW TUGEND   DIRECTED BY DWIGHT LITTLE

ISBN 0-590-25228-3

12 11 10 9 8 7 6 5 4 3 2   5 6 7 8 9/9 0/0

Printed in the U.S.A.   01

First Scholastic printing, July 1995

FREE WILLY 2

THE ADVENTURE HOME

Chapter 1

The three small whales hurried to catch up with the larger one, their mother. But Catspaw was far ahead of her children, slicing through the ocean's surface as if cutting a path for them to follow.

The whales were frolicking, breaking into the air, shooting water from their spouts, and splashing back down into the sea as they went. They called to each other with a series of throaty clicks and deep-bellied whines. *Whalesong*.

They were a family.

The shyest one, Luna, had a white patch in the shape of a crescent on her dorsal fin. She stayed close to her mother, chattering away as if fearful of being abandoned or of being carried away by the strong currents of the sea.

The others, the two brothers, were more confident. They were less afraid of the sea. Littlespot, with his single black marking under his chin, was the youngest and the smallest of the three. For the last several miles Littlespot had been dogging his older brother, mimicking his every move. No matter how fast the older swam, or how high he jumped, Littlespot remained unshakable.

The older one was the largest of Catspaw's three children. He had three black spots on his neck and a bent dorsal fin.

His name was Willy.

Although he was acting irritated at the taunts of young Littlespot, deep down Willy enjoyed this game of monkey-see-monkey-do. There had been a time, not that long before, when it was possible that Willy might never have seen Littlespot or the other members of his family again.

Two years earlier a great rumble had shaken the sea and a dark shadow had covered the sun. A many-tentacled shroud had trapped him and yanked him away from his family. He had been taken to a place where many eyes had watched him, laughed at him. It was the place where he could not breathe, where he was certain he was going to die.

But then came the special eyes. The soft ones. The ones that looked at him with compassion. With love. The ones with the hand that touched his tongue and stroked his snout. A sound often came into his mind from those days. The haunting sound of his human friend Jesse's harmonica.

Willy playfully jumped, breaching the water's surface, challenging Littlespot to keep up with him. Then, as soon as his little brother got close, Willy dove deep into the sea to try and lose him.

Littlespot dove after his big brother. Once submerged he could see Willy's sleek form pushing further into the dark depths of the sea. After a few moments Willy seemed to vanish. Littlespot brought himself to a stop and watched the stillness of the sea. He had lost the game again. Willy was nowhere to be found. Now Littlespot would have to return to the surface and wait. He knew that in a few moments Willy would return and the game would start again.

Littlespot looked up at the hazy splotch of sunlight that diffused across the ocean's surface. He began to move toward it when suddenly he heard a great roar. The water rippled all around him and a long shadow cut across his path.

Littlespot became frightened. He was pushed to and fro by the thick currents made by this new presence. Whatever it was, it was bigger and more powerful than anything he had ever seen before.

Just then he felt something nudge him from behind. It was Willy. Willy guided him away from the roaring shadow to a section of the sea where the sunlight could still be seen. Together the two brothers broke the surface of the water and rejoined their mother and sister, both of whom had been anxiously waiting for their return.

In the distance Willy could see the thing that had frightened Littlespot so. He had seen such a thing before. It floated on the surface of the sea and was powered by an unseen fin that roared as it went. It carried many tiny creatures, like the ones Willy remembered laughing at him two years before, when he thought he was going to die.

The thing was a ship. And the creatures were men.

Willy knew he had to keep away from ships and men. And he had to keep his family away from them as well.

Somehow he knew he could never let himself be captured by them again.

Chapter 2

Jesse stood at the helm of the boat, his hand on the throttle. Glen Greenwood, his foster father, stood beside him, watching him, making sure the boy was keeping a steady hand on the controls.

"The throttle has three positions," explained Glen. "Straight up and down is neutral, down is reverse, up is forward."

Jesse kept his hand steady in the up position.

"With a boat you're either in gear or out of gear," continued Glen. "So you need to shift quickly to get going or you'll grind metal on metal."

Glen took over the throttle and demonstrated. "Once you're in gear," he concluded, "you can ease it forward to accelerate. Jesse, pay attention."

But Jesse's eyes had drifted away from the controls to something off midship.

He grabbed a pair of high-powered binoculars from the dashboard and brought them up, craning his neck for a better look.

Then he jumped overboard, leaving the binoculars behind, landing feet first on the Greenwoods' cement driveway.

Jesse took a few steps forward, peering down the street. Then he found what he was looking for. There were three girls, each one riding a bicycle. They were all very beautiful. And they were riding straight toward him.

Jesse's mouth went dry and his heart began to beat faster.

Jesse recognized the girls from school, and waved at them. They all smiled and waved back flirtatiously.

It had been nearly two years since Glen and Annie Greenwood had officially become his foster parents. Now, at fourteen, he seemed to be just getting used to the idea. Still, he felt different from most of the other kids at school. Most of the ones he knew had had the same parents all their lives. He felt different. Sometimes he even felt as if he weren't as good as the other kids. He tried keeping the fact that he was a foster child a secret, afraid of what the other kids might think of him if they knew.

More often than not, however, his friends at school didn't seem to think less of Jesse. In fact, some of them thought it was pretty cool. Many of them, they'd often confess, wished they could trade in their parents for a set of new ones. Particularly ones as cool as Glen and Annie.

Jesse soon found himself drifting to meet the girls at the curb. He walked slowly, so he would look smooth — instead of nervous.

"Hey, Jesse. You coming down to the water tonight?" asked one of the girls with a friendly smile. "Big bonfire."

"I wish," said Jesse, shifting his weight anxiously. "But I have packing to do. Getting ready for vacation."

The girls glanced at each other. They were clearly disappointed.

"Too bad," said the girl that had spoken to him. "See you when you get back."

And with that the three girls spun their bikes around and rode off.

"Yeah," muttered Jesse with quiet disappointment. But it was too late. The girls couldn't hear him. They had already disappeared around a corner at the end of the street.

No matter, Jesse thought to himself with a shrug. Probably better this way. Still, he couldn't resist smiling. At least he knew the girls liked him. Besides, he was packing for a trip where, if he was lucky, he might get to see Willy again.

He turned and jaunted victoriously toward his house. That's when he noticed the car parked at the curb. He knew the car well. It belonged to Dwight Mercer, the social worker who had first introduced him to the Greenwoods two years ago.

Jesse wasn't surprised that Dwight was paying a visit. Social workers paid periodic visits to kids placed in foster homes just to make sure everything was going all right.

As far as Jesse was concerned everything was going great. At first he was suspicious of the Greenwoods. He used to wonder why they wanted a troublemaker like him around. But that quickly changed. After a time he came to trust the young couple. He even came to understand them.

He learned that Glen had been a lot like him growing up: always in trouble, always looking for a fight. Then Glen met Annie. She was tender and understanding and it made him want to change. He was able to love Annie, but after they were married they found out that they couldn't have children. Having a family was important to them, however. So they decided to look into adoption. They could have adopted an infant, but Annie met Dwight Mercer when she was writing some articles for the local paper on the Cooperton Juvenile Home. She learned a lot about foster care and the young kids that went in and out of there looking for a real family to live with. Annie and Glen decided to provide a foster home for one of them. The one they chose was Jesse.

Occasionally Jesse would still wonder about his birth mother. He used to worry about her more. But as he grew older he began to realize that much of what Dwight had said about her was true. She was troubled. She had made the decision to give

Jesse up. There was nothing Jesse could do to change that, even if he ever did find out where she was.

For now, Jesse was happy with things just the way they were.

Jesse hurried up the driveway and entered the house. Glen and Annie were standing in the living room. Dwight rose from the couch as soon as Jesse entered.

"Hey, Dwight." Jesse greeted him with a smile. "Didn't see you come in."

"You were busy," said Dwight.

"I'm starving," Jesse told Annie. "All that boating makes me hungry. You staying for supper, Dwight?"

Dwight shook his head. Suddenly Jesse realized that something was wrong. Terribly wrong. There had to be. He was the only happy person in the room.

"What?" he asked them.

Annie approached him and tenderly placed her arm on his.

"Jesse, sit down," she said.

"Why?" asked Jesse, confused.

"I'm sorry, Jesse," said Dwight. "We have some bad news."

Jesse took a step back. He felt a shiver tingle down his spine.

"They found your mother," Annie finally said. "In New York City. I'm afraid she's passed away."

"*What?*" asked Jesse. He couldn't believe it.

"I'm so sorry," said Dwight.

"No," said Jesse. He *refused* to believe it. "No! You're wrong!"

"Jesse — " Annie started, reaching her hand out to his again.

Jesse yanked his hand away. "I should have gone to look for her," he said, his voice filled with pain.

"She didn't want to be found," Dwight reminded him.

"I should have tried to help her," insisted Jesse, trying to fight back tears.

"There's nothing you could have done," said Glen.

"It's not too late," said Dwight.

Jesse looked at Dwight. "What's that supposed to mean?" he asked angrily.

Dwight threw a glance to both Annie and Glen. Then he took a step toward Jesse.

"Your mom still needs your help, Jesse," he explained in a very careful tone of voice. "Because she left somebody behind. You have a brother. Half-brother, actually. Eight years old."

"I don't want a brother," Jesse replied scornfully.

Glen, Annie, and Dwight stared helplessly at Jesse. For a moment he felt almost like he did two years ago. Everybody used to stare at him because they didn't understand him.

And they weren't understanding him now.

"Don't you get it?" he shouted at them. He was shaking. "I don't want a brother! I want my mom back!"

Once again Annie reached out to comfort Jesse. He pulled away again and this time ran out of the house, slamming the front door behind him as he went.

Jesse ran down the street, turned the corner, and kept running. He wanted to keep going forever. If he ran he wouldn't have to think. If he stopped to think it would bring too much pain.

Before long he was running out of breath. Without realizing it he had come to one of his favorite places. It was the pier that looked out over the harbor. He came to a stop at the end of the pier, his chest heaving. His eyes were wet with tears, but he wasn't sure if that was from the wind that had been ripping across his face or the sadness he was feeling inside.

He sat down at the edge of the pier and allowed his legs to dangle over its side. Then he stared out to sea.

Chapter 3

After a few moments Jesse heard some footsteps approach him from behind. He didn't have to turn around to know that they belonged to Glen. He didn't take his eyes off the horizon even as Glen sat down beside him.

"How could she ditch me and then have another kid?" Jesse said through tight, angry lips. "Why did she keep him and not me?"

Glen looked at Jesse helplessly. "I don't know," he replied.

"I really thought I would see her again, Glen. I thought if I was really good, I would get her back."

"Take it from me, Jesse," said Glen. "You're good."

Jesse brought his knee up and braced his chin against it. "I don't know what to do," he said. "I don't want to let go of her."

"You don't have to let go of her," said Glen. "She's a part of you."

Jesse's eyes began to water. A tear fell and soaked through the knee of his jeans. This time he knew they were tears of sadness. He quickly turned his head so Glen couldn't see.

"It's the cold air," he lied. "It makes my eyes run."

"That's okay," said Glen. "I get that, too."

For a moment neither one said a word. It had taken them two years to get close, to become a family. Now it looked like they would have to go through all that again.

"Your brother's going to come stay with us for a couple of weeks," Glen finally said. "Annie worked it out with Dwight. It's called Kinship Care and it's the law. You're his only known relative. He's going to stay with us until Dwight can place him with a permanent family."

"Or until Annie falls in love with him and never lets him leave," said Jesse, only half joking.

"Exactly," Glen agreed with a knowing nod.

"This stinks," groaned Jesse.

"Tell me about it," smirked Glen. "He's related to you, isn't he?"

Jesse couldn't help but smile. Things were good between him and Glen now, but they hadn't started out that way. In the beginning, two years before, Jesse had wanted no part of a foster family. All he wanted was to survive from day to day, even if it meant living from hand to mouth. The purpose for that, he used to reason, was to wait for the day his mother would come back for him.

But she never came back for him. And now he knew she never would.

Glen was there now. And so was Annie. In his mind his mother was just a phantom memory. She was not something he could ever reach out and touch. Glen and Annie were different. They were there every day. He could talk to them, exchange thoughts and ideas. They would listen to him and take his thoughts seriously. They cared about him. And he cared about them, too. But even more than that, he trusted them. If Glen and Annie thought the best thing was to take in his half-brother, Jesse supposed it would have to be okay with him, too.

Glen pulled something out of his pocket and handed it to him. It was Jesse's harmonica. He had dropped it just before running out of the house.

"What about our vacation?" asked Jesse as he and Glen walked away from the docks.

"What about it?"

"You want to bring him on our trip? A total stranger?"

"We'll still do everything we planned," promised Glen. "A little fishing. Visit Randolph at his job. Camp out. It'll still be fun."

"You really believe that?" asked Jesse warily.

Glen thought for a moment. "Ask me in a couple of days," he said. "Hey, you play any blues on that thing?"

Suddenly, without knowing why, Jesse began to smile. Then he put the harmonica to his lips and began to blow.

*   *   *

At the very same moment that Glen and Jesse were walking away from the pier, a boat was moving slowly through the choppy black waters of the Pacific Ocean. The boat was a maritime research vessel. That it specialized in the study of whales could be determined by the insignia of the Orca Institute that was spread across its side. Below the symbol was the name of the boat. *The Natselane*.

Randolph Ketchikan Johnson stood on the bridge of *The Natselane*. He was a tall, broad-shouldered man with straight black hair and a dark complexion. His cheekbones were set high on his face on either side of a strong, slightly curved nose. His blue eyes watched the sea.

A few minutes before, he thought he heard something from out at sea. It was the sound of whalesong. It was Randolph's job to seek out pods of whales and identify them for the records of the Orca Institute. Only this time the whalesong sounded hauntingly familiar. He was sure he had heard it somewhere before.

He raised his binoculars to his eyes and peered through, but saw nothing.

Below deck, Randolph's teenaged assistant activated a tape recorder. Soon the plaintive chatter from out at sea came through the ship's loudspeaker. The assistant made certain she recorded the sounds at the perfect levels.

Within seconds Randolph came racing down the steps and into the recording room. He brushed right past his assistant and took over the controls of the recording console. He began to rewind the tape and search for the recorded whalesong.

"What is it?" asked the assistant, sensing Randolph's excitement.

Randolph did not respond. Instead he stopped the tape and hit "play." The sounds of whalesong came through like a chorus. Next, he adjusted several filters. One by one the various whales fell silent until there was just one whale's voice.

He recognized the whale's voice instantly. "Willy," he muttered with a smile. A very big smile.

Chapter 4

That evening after dinner Jesse went up to his room, popped a CD into his stereo rack system, and stuffed his head between a pair of well-insulated headphones. Then he turned the volume on nearly full, picked up his guitar, and sat on his bed to play along as the music began.

Once the music started he couldn't hear anything else. Not the sound of the dishwasher running downstairs in the kitchen, or the sound of the news magazine show Glen was watching in the living room.

He especially couldn't hear the sounds of Dwight's car as it pulled into the Greenwoods' driveway, the driver and passenger

960059

doors of the car opening and slamming shut, or the front bell when Dwight rang.

Not hearing any of that was what Jesse wanted most just then. He wanted just a few more minutes of being the only foster son the Greenwoods had. Or at least having it sound as if he was.

Downstairs, Annie and Glen opened the front door. Dwight was standing there with his arm around the shoulder of an eight-year-old boy. The boy wore an Army fatigue jacket and blue jeans and his hair was tousled.

"Glen, Annie," said Dwight. "I'd like you to meet Elvis. Elvis, these are the Greenwoods."

"Come in," Annie said to Elvis in her sweetest voice. "Come in."

Elvis took one step inside the house and quickly scanned the hallway and what he could see of the living room. Then he shrugged, unimpressed.

"Are you rich?" he asked Glen.

"Elvis — " cautioned Dwight.

"Dwight said you were rich," said Elvis and he stepped further into the foyer.

"I never said that," Dwight said to Glen

with embarrassment. Glen smiled with understanding.

"I told Dwight I could only stay with people who are loaded," continued Elvis. "So it wouldn't be too much of an adjustment."

"Well," replied Glen. "I guess that's going to be one of life's little disappointments."

There was an uncomfortable silence. For a long moment nobody said a word. Finally, Annie brought her hands together.

"Well," she said to Elvis. "I'll see what's keeping your brother."

Annie went upstairs and knocked on Jesse's door, but there was no answer. When she let herself in she noticed that Jesse was on the bed listening to his headphones, strumming his guitar, his eyes closed. He was totally oblivious to her presence.

Annie crossed the room and turned off the power on Jesse's stereo.

Once the music stopped Jesse opened his eyes, but continued to stare straight up at the ceiling. He instinctively knew that Annie was in the room. And just as instinctively, he knew why.

"What's he look like?" Jesse asked without even looking over at her.

"Why don't you come down and see for yourself?" Annie suggested.

"I don't feel like it."

Annie paused. She had a feeling this wasn't going to be easy. "Jesse," she began cautiously. "Why don't you talk to him? Maybe you could learn something."

"Like what?"

"He's been living with your mom for the last eight years," said Annie. "You tell me."

Jesse sat up and looked at Annie. She was right, he realized. He had never really known his mother. Now the only person who knew anything about her was standing downstairs waiting to meet him.

Jesse followed Annie downstairs, descending slowly, apprehensive of what he might find when he reached the bottom. Dwight and Glen were standing in the front hall watching him as he approached.

Finally, Jesse came face-to-face with Elvis. The two boys looked each other up and down. Then they stared into each other's faces. They instantly felt something familiar about each other. It was almost as if they had met a long time ago, but couldn't remember where or when.

All of a sudden the two boys dropped their fascinated expressions and looked away from each other.

"Hi," said Jesse. His voice was cold and unfriendly.

Elvis shrugged. "Whatever," he replied and continued to look over the house.

Annie and Glen watched as the two boys drifted away from each other. Then they looked at each other and exchanged expressions of helplessness.

Chapter 5

The next morning, when Elvis got up, he heard some movement outside in the Greenwoods' driveway. He strolled out and saw Annie loading up the truck with luggage. Jesse and Glen were attaching the fishing boat to the rear of the truck.

Elvis sat down on the lawn and watched and waited. He had rejected the thought of helping the Greenwoods. This seemed right to him. After all, he reasoned, what were the Greenwoods to him? He wasn't part of their family. Why should he act as if he was? So what if Jesse was his half-brother, he thought? What does that mean anyway? A half-brother isn't a whole brother. Anyway, he thought as he watched Jesse move nimbly between the boat and the truck, maybe they weren't even brothers at all. To him they didn't look anything alike.

Now many quick and elusive memories of his mother flooded Elvis's head. In his mind he knew that she was dead, that she had gone away and was never coming back. But in his heart, he felt differently. He had a suspicion that one day his mother would find her way back to him. He decided he would be ready when that day came. He wouldn't be like Jesse. He wouldn't abandon her for some other parents. No, he would be a loyal son and wait.

It took another hour for the Greenwoods to finish loading up the truck. Annie had taken Elvis's suitcase and packed it in, too. He had wanted to stop her, but was too smart for that. He knew he'd get into big trouble if he tried to run away while the Greenwoods went on vacation, so he decided to play along. It was only a matter of time before his mom would come back to him, he decided. Until then he had to survive.

So when everyone piled into the truck

Elvis went along. He sat in the backseat with Jesse, while Glen drove and Annie plotted their route with a state map.

After traveling for nearly half an hour Annie realized there was a dead silence coming from the backseat. She turned around to see Jesse and Elvis staring out of their windows doing their best not to look interested in each other.

"So," Annie said to Elvis, trying to break the silence. "How'd you get a name like Elvis, Elvis?"

Elvis continued to stare out the window. "My mom," he said flatly. He was clearly not interested in talking.

"Hey," said Glen. "That's how I got my name, too."

Elvis didn't laugh. "Whatever," he said. "I'm going to be a big movie star just like my dad."

"Right," said Jesse, hiding a doubtful smirk.

"My dad, Al Pacino," insisted Elvis. "My friends call me Godfather."

"You have friends?" asked Jesse.

"Fans."

"Give me a break."

Annie threw a helpless look to Glen as

she turned back around. It felt like two years ago all over again.

Glen turned the car off the thruway and began heading west. After a while the ocean could be seen through the windows. Not long after that the harbor appeared.

As soon as he saw the water Elvis's eyes widened with excitement. "Hey!" he exclaimed. "The ocean! My mom loved the ocean! My mom was born at sea, you know."

"That's interesting," said Annie without even turning around. She had already heard enough of Elvis's outrageous claims.

"On an aircraft carrier," insisted Elvis as if trying to tweak Annie's interest. "Nobody's supposed to know that. It's classified."

Jesse faced Elvis. He had heard enough. "Do you come with a remote?" he asked the boy sharply.

Elvis suddenly became very quiet. These people were typical, he thought. First they try to get you to talk, then they don't believe anything you say.

He stared back out the window. The ocean was getting closer. To Elvis it looked like an endless blue-green pasture ready to be played in. He couldn't wait to get there, even though he really didn't know why.

Glen pulled the truck up to the vehicle entry level of the ferry boat and, along with several other families and their cars, waited patiently as the ferry from Friday Harbor pulled in and lowered its ramp. Once the ramp was in place Glen slowly drove to an available space on the lower deck of the ferry.

When they were safely parked, Glen and Annie guided Jesse and Elvis out of the truck and to the upper deck. The upper deck was slowly becoming crowded with passengers. Many leaned against the railing, waiting for the ferry to take off. Jesse and Elvis did the same. Both boys felt a rush of excitement as they heard the ferry's motor kick in. Then the huge, hulking craft pushed off through the foamy sea waters and began heading back across the channel.

Moving out of earshot of Jesse, Annie turned to Glen.

"You talk to Randolph again?" she asked.

"He's going to meet us at the campground," Glen replied, nodding. "He wants to take Jesse out on the water by himself."

In the meantime Jesse and Elvis continued to look out at sea. In the distance they could see islands growing larger as the ferry approached them.

Jesse glanced over at Elvis. For the first time since they met he began to study the boy's face. There was something familiar about it. He knew that from the beginning. But it wasn't just his features that seemed familiar. It was an attitude. A sense of experience. For a fleeting moment Jesse felt he had something in common with Elvis. He couldn't take his eyes off the boy.

"What are you staring at?" asked Elvis without even looking at his brother.

"What are *you* staring at?" responded Jesse.

"A bunch of water."

"Shows what you know," said Jesse.

"Is there an amusement park on this island?" Elvis asked.

"No," replied Jesse. "There's a whale spotting station."

"You mean where they paint spots on whales?" asked Elvis. He clearly had no idea what whale spotting was.

"Yes," answered Jesse, rolling his eyes at the dumb question.

Suddenly the deck came alive with a flurry of activity. All the passengers had rushed toward one spot of the railing, each struggling to look over the heads of the others. Some were pointing. Others were snapping pictures. There was something going on at sea.

Jesse and Elvis joined the excited crowd, squeezing through until they reached a clear spot at the rail. Now they had an unobstructed view of what everyone else was seeing.

It was a pod of orcas. Six of them to be exact. And they were surfing the waves made by the thrust of the ferry as it pushed through the water.

Elvis had never seen anything like it before. The whales seemed to move together as if in a dance. Their long, sleek forms remained equidistant from each other as they rode the waves. There was an exuberance about them. A happiness. They seemed to be showing off to the people on the ferry.

Then Elvis looked over at Jesse, whose eyes were fixed on the dancing whales, but whose thoughts seemed to be someplace else. A gentle smile had come over Jesse's face. It was a gentleness Elvis had not seen before in the older boy. For the first time since meeting Jesse, Elvis wanted to know more about him. What was it about the sight of the whale pod that was making Jesse smile so?

Elvis wished he could find out.

Chapter 6

"Jesse!" Glen called out.

Jesse was standing a few yards from the campsite on a ridge that overlooked the water. From that position he could see all up and down the straits and across to the other islands. It was a magnificent view that made him feel as if he were looking down on the whole world. Below the ridge was a crescent-shaped beach with crags and sharp rocks jutting all about it. A few feet down the beach was a wooden dock with a road leading to it from the hills. That, he knew, was where he and the Greenwoods would take their boat and set off each day to go fishing. He was looking forward to that.

"Jesse!" Glen called out again. "We need your help!"

Jesse returned to the clearing where Glen and Annie were setting up camp. The campsite had come provided with a picnic table and a low barbecue, and Glen and Annie were setting up two tents that they had brought from home. The larger one was for them. The smaller one was for Jesse and Elvis.

Jesse cringed at the thought of sharing his tent with Elvis. He had just gotten used to the idea of having foster parents. Why did he have to share them?

Everything about Elvis annoyed Jesse. The kid was a compulsive liar. Jesse didn't like that. He acted as if he were more important than anyone else. Jesse didn't like that, either. On top of everything else, Elvis hadn't lifted a finger to help anyone since the vacation began. Even now, as Glen struggled to hammer tent stakes into the ground, Elvis was just standing on the side watching.

But Jesse knew there was something

more that bothered him about Elvis, something he couldn't quite put his finger on. It was something in his face and in the way he moved. It was the gnawing familiarity that bothered Jesse. It was as if Elvis was a younger version of himself. Jesse wasn't sure if he liked that. He had always thought of himself as special and unique. Seeing his own eyes in Elvis's suddenly made him wonder if he really wasn't that special after all.

He wished Elvis had never been born.

As soon as Jesse dropped his gear in the small tent he headed over to help Glen put up the larger one. Just then a pickup truck turned down the trail leading into the campsite. Jesse watched as it came to a stop and Randolph got out.

"Hey, Jess!" called Randolph. "Look at you! You must have grown six inches!"

Jesse ran to his tall, Native American friend. He hadn't seen Randolph since two summers before, when he worked as his assistant at the Northwest Adventure Park.

"Four and a half," replied Jesse with pride as he shook Randolph's hand.

"Since breakfast," added Glen as he and

Annie approached Randolph and greeted him.

"Glen, Annie," smiled Randolph. "It's nice to see you."

Just then Randolph caught sight of Elvis, who was standing a few steps behind the rest.

"Is this your brother?" Randolph asked Jesse.

Jesse didn't answer. Elvis, on the other hand, extended his hand to shake Randolph's.

"My name's Elvis," he said. "I'm half Apache."

Jesse groaned. Glen and Annie rolled their eyes. Elvis was lying again.

But Randolph took Elvis's hand and stared into his face, studying him. There was a lot of Jesse in that face, he realized. A lot of the rebel.

"Pleased to meet you, Elvis," said Randolph without letting go of the boy's hand. Then his tone became dark and serious. "The Apaches are the sworn enemy of my people."

Elvis's eyes went wide with fear. "Really?" he asked timidly.

Randolph let go of Elvis's hand and

smiled as he shook his head no. Everyone tried not to laugh when Elvis let out a huge sigh of relief.

Randolph swung his arm around Jesse's shoulders. "Come on," he said. "We're going for a ride."

"Where we going?" asked Jesse.

"To do some whale spotting."

Jesse threw a glance at Glen and Annie silently asking their permission to go. Apparently they had already given it, because they were nodding and smiling by the time Randolph had started up the truck.

With a huge smile Jesse opened the passenger side door of the truck and started to climb in. Before he could close the door, however, Elvis came running up from behind.

No way, Jesse thought as he slammed the door in Elvis's face. And with that he settled into his seat as Randolph shifted gears and drove the pickup back up the road and away from the campsite.

"I've got a couple of surprises for you," said Randolph a few minutes later. He reached into a backpack and pulled out a beautifully carved wooden orca. Then he handed it to Jesse. "Here. For you, from my village."

Jesse took the carving and studied it. The sleek whale was carved intricately, its teeth bared. There was something both powerful and mysterious about it. A long chain was attached to it.

"My people believe your soul lives here," said Randolph, touching a spot just below his chest. "When you wear the necklace, the orca is close to your spirit."

"This is great, Randolph," said Jesse. And it was. For the first time since leaving home Jesse was starting to feel good again. And seeing Randolph made him feel great. His thoughts drifted back to two years earlier. To the night he and a friend, runaways from the juvenile home, had snuck into the Northwest Adventure Park and vandalized one of the attractions, a huge water tank. A tank that was home to a magnificent orca called Willy.

Caught and returned to the juvenile home, Jesse's punishment was to clean up the mess he had made. Randolph was the seaquarium supervisor at the time, but he soon became more than that to Jesse.

At first Jesse thought it strange when

he felt he could actually communicate with the great whale in the tank. He thought it even stranger when he convinced himself that Willy wasn't the grouchy, unfriendly creature the seaquarium owners thought him to be. He was only lonely. Lonely for his family, from whom he had been separated months earlier.

The only one who didn't think Jesse's feeling was strange was Randolph. It was as if Randolph knew that Jesse and Willy were somehow connected by some common bond. A bond that may have been as ancient as time itself.

"I've missed having you around, Jesse," said Randolph, echoing Jesse's private thoughts. "I don't know many people who have what you have."

"What do I have?" asked Jesse skeptically.

"Medicine roots," replied Randolph. "It makes you special."

They drove in silence for a moment.

"It was the best thing I've ever done in my life," said Randolph. "Setting Willy free."

Jesse smiled. He and Randolph were

thinking the exact same thing. "Me, too," he said. "Have you seen him?"

"Seen Willy? No."

"Then what's the second surprise?" asked Jesse. He was disappointed. Earlier Randolph had said he had a couple of surprises for Jesse. The necklace was one. Jesse had hoped a reunion with Willy was the other.

He supposed he had been wrong because Randolph never answered him and instead continued to drive the rest of the way in silence.

Chapter 7

The Natselane sat at anchor next to a long, wooden dock. After parking the pickup truck next to a log cabin outpost bearing the insignia of the Orca Institute, Randolph led Jesse down along the dock to the boat. Then he climbed aboard the bridge and checked some gauges.

"Take up that line and we'll be on our way!" Jesse heard Randolph shout.

At first Jesse thought Randolph was talking to him. But a second later, a girl about Jesse's own age popped out from the starboard side of the ship. Then she crossed over to the aft line, untied it, and jumped back aboard.

The girl wore a T-shirt and cutoff jeans. She was about Jesse's height and her full head of brown hair was stuffed inside a baseball cap that sat slightly askew on her head. From where he stood Jesse saw that she had brown eyes and a small, roundish nose.

Jesse couldn't take his eyes off of her.

"I hope she's the second surprise," Jesse said to Randolph.

"I'll ignore that," said Randolph as he checked some more gauges on the ship's control panel.

But Jesse couldn't ignore the girl. "Aren't you going to introduce me?" he asked Randolph in an almost pleading tone.

"No," Randolph said firmly. "Come on upstairs and ride along with me. I'll help you steer."

Jesse followed Randolph halfway up a short flight of winding spiral stairs. He nearly hit his head trying to catch a glimpse of the girl. He was still trying as he pulled the line on deck.

"Who is she?" he asked.

"She's my orca spotter," replied Randolph before disappearing to the upper level.

43

Jesse followed Randolph to the upper level, the ship's helm. Randolph turned on the ship's motor. Jesse felt a powerful rumble surge through his body. Then Randolph turned the steering wheel and began guiding *The Natselane* away from the dock, down a narrow channel, and out into the open sea.

No sooner had they gotten under way than Jesse began craning his neck. Only he wasn't looking out at sea. He was looking toward the back of the boat, still trying to see the girl.

That's when Randolph shoved a huge pair of binoculars into Jesse's hands.

"Keep your eyes peeled," he ordered Jesse and pointed out at sea.

Red-faced, Jesse brought the binoculars up to his eyes and looked out toward the horizon. But there was nothing there except the expanse of the sea as it met the sky. Bored, he aimed the binoculars in a different direction, toward the back of the boat. Here he had an unobstructed view of the girl as she tended to some equipment.

Almost instantly Jesse's view was obstructed by Randolph's massive hand.

"Give me a break, Jesse," pleaded Randolph. "She's my goddaughter."

"What's that mean?" asked Jesse as he lowered the binoculars.

"That means she's not my daughter," explained Randolph. His voice had a certain warning tone to it. "But she's *like* a daughter to me. I look out for her. Nadine!"

At the sound of her name the girl walked over to the helm, brushing past Jesse as she did. Jesse held his breath. She was more beautiful up close than from far away. And she smelled great, too, as if she had spent her whole life outside and near the sea.

"Nadine, this is Jess," Randolph told the girl. "Jesse, Nadine."

"Hi," said Jesse nervously. He could hardly bring himself to look her in the eye.

Nadine quickly studied Jesse's face. "Hello," she said. But there was something unfriendly in the way she said it, as if she had already decided that she didn't like Jesse.

Randolph handed the helm over to Nadine and told Jesse to follow him downstairs. Once below deck, Randolph led

Jesse to the recording equipment console and started up the tape cassette player.

"Listen to this," he told Jesse.

The sounds of ocean depths, thick and strange, came over the speakers. Then Randolph began adjusting the filters until the only thing that could be heard was the sound of whales' voices.

"We've been tracking this pod all the way up the Pacific Coast," explained Randolph. "Each pod has its own dialect, like an accent, which helps us ID them from a distance."

Randolph adjusted the filters some more. Soon there was only one whale's voice that could be heard.

Jesse could feel his whole body go limp when he heard the voice. He recognized it instantly.

"Randolph . . ." he began with a start.

"I didn't want to tell you till I knew for sure," said Randolph. "But we sighted Willy's pod in these waters over the last couple of days."

"And Willy, too, right?" Jesse asked excitedly. "We have to find him, Randolph."

"That's why I brought you here, Jesse," Randolph explained. "But I have to warn you, Willy's been living in the wild, in the open sea. There's no telling if he'll even remember us."

"He'll remember," Jesse said with dead certainty. "He has to remember."

"There's no telling how tame he'll be," warned Randolph. "There are no guarantees."

Jesse didn't care about the warning. "We have to try," he said.

Randolph nodded in agreement. "We have nothing to lose," he said.

Then both Randolph and Jesse smiled.

Very big smiles.

Chapter 8

An hour later Jesse was standing at the helm of *The Natselane* when he caught sight of something through his binoculars. Randolph, who was standing next to him, didn't need binoculars to recognize the sight.

"A pod of white-side dolphins," Randolph told Jesse. "Lucky ones. The unlucky ones are in aquariums all over the country."

Nadine, who was a few feet away monitoring the underwater sounds registered on a hydrophone, recognized the dolphins, too.

"Their normal life span can reach twenty-five years," she added with a certain amount of authoritativeness. "But in captivity, they won't live past the age of four."

Jesse was impressed with Nadine. Not only did she handle her shipboard duties confidently and professionally, but she seemed to have a broad knowledge of marine life as well.

Randolph signaled to Nadine, slicing his hand through the air. Nadine understood the signal and immediately cut the boat's engine. Now the boat was silent and drifting. Then Randolph turned up the volume on the underwater hydrophone and waited, listening.

Jesse listened, too. He heard the din and grind of a distant ship's engines.

"Sounds like a power boat," said Randolph, as he listened to the faraway ship. "That's a tanker."

Close by the distant ship a series of squeaks and squeals could be heard.

"Orcas?" asked Jesse hopefully.

"No orcas," replied Randolph.

Jesse frowned with disappointment.

"Let's try Turner's Point," Randolph said to Nadine. "Maybe they're out having lunch." With that he threw Jesse an encouraging wink and signaled Nadine to start up the engines again.

In a few minutes *The Natselane* was underway again. Nadine had gone to the upper deck for a more unobstructed view of the sea. Jesse wanted to follow her, but decided to wait. He didn't have the courage. After a few minutes, however, he knew he would have to say something to her then or he never would.

He climbed to the upper deck and stood beside Nadine, who was at the railing looking out to sea.

"So," Jesse said after an uncomfortable moment.

"Buttons on ice cream, see if they stick," replied Nadine.

"What?" asked Jesse, a bit confused. All of a sudden Nadine had a playful tone in her voice.

"Sew buttons on ice cream, see if they stick," Nadine repeated. "It's an expression. Somebody says 'so,' and you say — "

"Buttons on ice cream, see if they stick?" repeated Jesse. "That's pretty good."

"Yeah," Nadine said with a shrug. "It's like a joke."

Jesse shrugged, too. He didn't really find the joke all that funny, but at least he wasn't afraid to talk to Nadine anymore. He was about to ask her where she had learned so much about marine life when they were suddenly interrupted.

"J-pod!" they heard Randolph call from the helm.

Jesse knew what that meant. Orcas. He and Nadine exchanged excited glances and rushed to Randolph's side. Not more than thirty yards ahead a pod of orcas moved gracefully along, diving, spouting, surfacing.

"Let's get closer!" exclaimed Jesse.

"Can't," said Randolph. "We're required by law to keep our distance. A hundred yards."

"I count six, maybe seven," said Jesse as he counted the whales. "Randolph, look at the size of that one!"

He was pointing to one who was the biggest of the bunch. Randolph smiled. He recognized the whale instantly.

"That's Catspaw," said Randolph. "Willy's mother."

"Look!" shouted Nadine pointing toward the pod.

Suddenly three of the orcas dived below the surface and out of view. Was Willy one of them? Jesse had to know. He raced to the upper deck for a better view, but by the time he got there all the whales had disappeared.

"Was that them?" Jesse called down to Randolph.

"Too far away to tell, Jess," replied Randolph. "Could be Willy's brother and sister, Littlespot and Luna. The family pretty much sticks together."

Suddenly the whales broke the surface of the water again. Jesse brought his binoculars to his eyes and focused them. One of the whales arched and dived back under the surface.

"That one has a white patch on his fin," said Jesse.

"*Her* fin," corrected Randolph. "That's Willy's sister, Luna."

By now Nadine had turned *The Natselane* in the direction of the whales. That's when Jesse saw another one of the whales break the water's surface. The graceful movement of the great creature was so familiar to Jesse he recognized it even before seeing its bent dorsal fin.

Jesse dropped his binoculars on the floor. His heart leaped into his throat.

"Willy," he whispered to himself. Then he shouted: "Willy!"

But Willy was too far away to hear Jesse call.

Randolph raced over and handed Jesse a whistle. It was just like the whistle Jesse used two years earlier when he was training Willy at the Northwest Adventure Park.

Jesse instantly knew what to do. He blew a series of short sounds out of the whistle.

But by now the whale pod had moved farther out to sea. Willy was too far away to hear anything. As he pulled the whistle away from his lips Jesse watched the last of the whales dive below the surface and disappear from view.

Then Jesse noticed that *The Natselane* was slowing down. In fact, its engines had been turned off. The ship was coming to a stop.

Jesse called down to Nadine at the helm.

"What are you doing?" he shouted angrily. "Why are we stopping?"

"It's getting late," Nadine replied matter-of-factly. "We have a long way back."

A look of deep disappointment showed across Jesse's face.

"They're hunting now, Jesse," said Randolph softly. "We can try again tomorrow."

Okay, thought Jesse, though he wished he could grab the helm himself and follow the whales right then. But he knew better than that. He remembered the first time he met Willy. It took a lot of patience to get Willy to trust him. He realized it would take the same kind of patience now.

"Why is Willy's fin still bent?" Jesse asked Randolph.

"The cartilage grew that way when he was in captivity," explained Randolph as he kicked *The Natselane*'s engine in and began steering her back toward the docks. "Now it will never change. Hey, at least it makes him easy to recognize."

Jesse smiled. "I would have recognized him anyway," he said with certainty.

And he was more than certain that Willy would recognize him as well.

Chapter 9

The Natselane was close to port when Jesse decided to try and talk to Nadine again. There was still so much he wanted to know about her.

He found her below deck. She was dutifully recording the time of the J-pod sighting into a special nautical notebook.

Jesse stood there for a few seconds, fidgeting with his hands, waiting for the right moment to say something, but he couldn't think of anything that sounded right. If only he could be certain that she liked him, but so far she acted as if she wouldn't care if he jumped overboard.

The seconds seemed to last an eternity

before Jesse realized he couldn't wait any longer.

"How long you been working for Randolph?" he asked so quietly he wasn't sure if Nadine could hear him.

"Since he got here," replied Nadine. "Two summers. But I've known him ever since I can remember. His dad and my dad were in the army together."

There was another awkward silence as Nadine got up and headed out on deck. But this time she brushed past Jesse as she went. And gave him a little smile as well.

Jesse smiled. Maybe Nadine liked him after all. He followed her out on deck and watched as she packed up some equipment.

"I worked with him one summer," he said.

"I know," replied Nadine without looking up at him.

"He told you about me?"

"Uh-huh."

Jesse smiled. Then Nadine turned around and looked Jesse straight in the eyes. She did this for a long moment, as if she were studying him the way she might a fish she had never seen before. Jesse suddenly felt uncomfortable and began fidgeting with his hands again.

"Did Randolph happen to mention to you that I have medicine roots?" Jesse blurted out, unable to think of anything else to say.

Nadine smirked. "So let me see 'em," she quipped.

"It's not something you have on you," explained Jesse. "It's inside you."

Nadine rolled her eyes at Jesse. That said volumes. Jesse blushed with embarrassment and decided he would wait for tomorrow before trying again to get to know her. Maybe tomorrow, he thought, maybe after she'd seen him and Willy together, maybe then she'd believe him.

"How's it goin'?" asked Glen. When Jesse returned to the campsite, Glen was sitting alone by the campfire sipping a cup of coffee.

"Randolph found Willy," replied Jesse.

Glen could sense Jesse's excitement. "Yeah," he said. "He mentioned something about that."

"It was so cool, Glen," Jesse said as he sat down and warmed himself by the fire.

"And I only saw him for a second, a million miles away, with binoculars!"

"That's pretty good, considering," said Glen. "It's been a long time since you've seen him."

"It must be great for him," said Jesse thoughtfully.

"To be with his family, you mean," said Glen.

"Yeah."

Jesse and Glen stared into the warm glow of the crackling fire. It was hypnotizing.

"Do you think he misses me?" asked Jesse after a moment.

"Jesse," replied Glen. "When you're in someone's heart, you stay there forever. Besides, you have your family, too. Just like Willy."

Jesse looked at Glen. He had gotten used to talking things through with the large, rugged-looking man. He often looked forward to it. Glen and Annie had worked hard to make him feel as if he were part of their family. It was a nice feeling.

A few feet away Annie emerged from Jesse's tent. Elvis was with her.

"I can't sleep on the ground," Jesse heard

Elvis say. Seeing Elvis made him think of what Glen had just said about being part of a family. Okay, the kid was a pain. And he was a fibber, too. But maybe he lied because he was scared. Just like Jesse was once. Jesse decided he would try and be more patient with Elvis, just the way Glen and Annie had been patient with him. And the way he had to be patient with Willy.

"We're all sleeping on the ground," Jesse told his brother as he began helping Annie roll out their sleeping bags.

"You have two pads and I only have one," said Elvis pointing to Jesse's sleeping bag.

"We're all supposed to have two pads," said Jesse. "But no one knew you were coming."

"I have a bad back," said Elvis insistently.

Jesse looked at Elvis skeptically.

"Jesse, why don't you let Elvis have the extra pad?" suggested Annie. "He's the guest after all."

Jesse nearly choked with incredulity as he pulled the extra pad from under his sleeping bag and tossed it to Elvis. Then Annie left. Afterwards the boys climbed into their sleeping bags and Jesse turned off the lamp. Now the tent was illuminated only by the white light of the full moon outside.

"You don't have a bad back, do you?" Jesse asked Elvis.

"I do so," insisted Elvis. "I get spasms. Which I got bungee jumping. In the Alps."

That was it, thought Jesse. He decided he didn't have enough patience for this. He sat up and drew an imaginary line down the center of the tent.

"See this line?" he asked Elvis.

"No."

"Cross it, I kill you."

Then Jesse lay back down.

"Glen and Annie told me all about you and Willy," said Elvis breaking a long silence.

"Go to sleep."

"Same exact thing happened to me two summers ago."

"Shut up!"

Elvis stopped talking, but he kept his eyes on Jesse who was looking up through an open flap of the tent, up at the bright full moon. Then he stretched a foot out across the ground.

"Is *this* the line you don't want me to

cross?" he asked in a challenging tone of voice.

"You're dead," warned Jesse.

"Or is *this* the line?" asked Elvis moving his foot even closer to Jesse.

At that Jesse jumped out of his sleeping bag and stormed out of the tent. He walked angrily and steadily across the campsite and toward the surrounding woods.

Glen was still at the campfire when Jesse walked past him.

"Where are you going?" asked Glen.

"Out of here!" shouted Jesse as he disappeared into the woods.

Glen started after Jesse, but stopped when he saw that Elvis had also emerged from the small tent.

"I'm sorry," said Elvis. He looked sorrowful.

"What did you do?" asked Glen.

"I crossed the line," replied Elvis. Glen could tell that Elvis was truly sorry for crossing the line.

Whatever that meant.

Jesse was still hot with rage as he walked down the craggy path that led to the dock. Once there he sat down and stared out at the black sea. The moonlight cast a shiny light across the gently rippling water. The rhythm of it calmed Jesse. After a while he took his harmonica out of his pocket and began to blow into it. The notes he played were sad and mournful.

After a while something stirred in the water beneath Jesse's feet. He stopped playing and looked down. Nothing. Jesse brought the harmonica back toward his mouth, but this time he lost his grip and the instrument slipped out of his hands and into the water.

Great, thought Jesse as he leaned over the edge of the pier and struggled to look for the harmonica. But it was gone. By now it was probably halfway toward the bottom of the sea.

Suddenly Jesse saw another movement from beneath the water's surface. The water rippled slowly, then more agitatedly. Something was rising from below. Something dark. Something big.

Chapter 10

Then it came, exploding up through the water's surface, its huge rubbery black head shaking exuberantly.

Water was splashing all around. Jesse was soaked through and through, his eyes blinded by the salty wetness.

Jesse rubbed his eyes hard trying to get the stinging water out of them. He couldn't see anything but he could hear the short repetitive chattering sounds that had once been so familiar to him. Finally, his vision cleared. Before him Willy had partially risen out of the water, his enormous, sharp tooth-filled mouth open in a wide smile.

"Willy!" Jesse shouted happily.

Willy responded by chattering even more wildly at the sound of Jesse's voice.

Jesse reached his hand out and tried to touch his old friend again, but Willy backed away as if challenging Jesse to jump into the water and play with him.

"Come here, Willy," said Jesse. "Come over here."

Willy bobbed closer to the dock, toward Jesse's outstretched hand. Jesse slowly reached out further until he was able to stroke Willy's shiny brow.

Jesse had been dreaming of this moment for two years. He could hardly believe it was actually happening.

"You've grown, haven't you?" Jesse asked Willy softly. Willy became calm at the feel of Jesse's hand and the gentle sound of the boy's voice. "I guess you've been eating pretty well out here, huh?"

Jesse's mind filled with images from two years before. He wondered if Willy could remember that far back. He decided to find out. He raised his hand and gave Willy the old "open mouth" signal. Willy responded immediately by opening his huge mouth, revealing Jesse's harmonica.

"Wow! You found it. Thanks boy," Jesse

said, taking the instrument from the orca's mouth. Jesse touched Willy's tongue and stroked it gently.

"I've missed you, boy," he told the whale. After a moment Jesse's thoughts wandered off in another direction. He became filled with sadness. Then he added, "I lost my mom."

Willy let out a sorrowful little wail as if he could sense the meaning of what Jesse had said.

"You have your family again," said Jesse. "It must feel great. Without my mom, I feel like I'm nobody. I'm all alone."

Jesse was surprised by his own words. Up until now he thought he had accepted that his mom was gone. He even thought he realized that he had held on to her too long. Now he knew that he had just been pushing certain feelings away. Ignoring them. He had lost his mom and it was like he had lost a part of himself.

Then a sound came drifting toward the dock. It was another whale calling from a distance out at sea.

"That's your mom calling, isn't it?" asked Jesse.

Jesse was right. Willy rolled over on his

side and waved his fin at Jesse. Then he turned his large sleek form around and moved back out to sea, back to his mother.

Jesse watched Willy swim away, savoring the sight until the whale finally disappeared from view.

So excited he could barely contain himself, Jesse ran back to the campsite. Glen and Annie were sitting at the campfire awaiting his return. They said nothing as Jesse sat down directly opposite them, his eyes still sparkling with excitement.

"You know what, Glen?" Jesse asked as he stared blissfully into the fire.

"What?"

"He *does* miss me."

Glen and Annie exchanged quizzical glances. Jesse smiled. He knew they had stayed up late because they were worried about him. They probably wanted to know why he had run away in the first place.

Funny thing was, Jesse realized, he could hardly remember why he had run away himself.

Chapter 11

By the time dusk had fallen, Captain Hans Nilson had checked his compass and marked his map three times while his helmsman looked on. Nilson looked worried. It was clear that his ship, *The Dakar*, was behind schedule. That wasn't good. Nilson had built his reputation by delivering shipments on time, no matter what the cost. And the companies that hired him paid extra for that reputation. He couldn't afford a single delay.

"What is it, sir?" asked the helmsman, although after serving under Captain Nilson for the last several years he already knew the answer.

"We lost time up north," replied Nilson. "We're behind."

"So Benbrook Oil gets its crude a day late," said the helmsman. "We've got plenty more."

Nilson threw the helmsman a stern look. The man ought to know better by now, he thought to himself.

"Do you know why I'm the captain of this ship, Kelly?" Nilson asked the helmsman.

Kelly lowered his eyes. "Yes, sir," he started. "I mean, no, sir." He knew that Nilson intended to tell him why.

"I'm captain of this ship because my ships always run on time," Nilson stated firmly. "Benbrook Oil does not look kindly on late deliveries. If we're late, we can all start looking for new jobs."

Suddenly a voice came crackling over the radio.

"*Dakar*," said the voice. "This is Seattle Traffic. We have a report of sixty-knot winds and reduced visibility at Smith Island. Over."

"Reducing speed to twelve knots," Kelly told his captain.

But Nilson stared Kelly down. "Maintain fifteen knots," he ordered. Nothing was going to make him late. Especially nature.

"But, sir," Kelly insisted. "Regulations on these waters — "

But the expression on Nilson's face was enough to cut Kelly off. Captain Nilson looked determined. Kelly decided he was obsessed.

Nilson turned back to his compass and maps. "I know these waters like the back of my hand," he said defiantly.

Chapter 12

Jesse held the flashlight high until it illuminated Elvis's sleeping face. It was late. Annie and Glen had finally put out the campfire and gone to bed. Jesse had gone to bed, too, but found he couldn't sleep. Something was gnawing at him.

He wasn't sure what made him get out of his sleeping bag and point the flashlight on his sleeping brother's face. There was something that had seemed familiar about Elvis ever since he arrived. Jesse felt determined to find out what it was.

He studied the boy's face in the soft yellow lamplight. In it he saw reminders of his own face. Something in the eyes, the nose, the lips. He also saw reminders of his mother's face, or what he remembered of it.

But he had seen these things before, when he first met Elvis, and several times since. What, then, was bothering him? He couldn't see it while the boy slept. Sleeping, Elvis looked soft and gentle, even helpless. Jesse thought of the many lies Elvis had told since they met. Now, in the silence of his own thoughts, he couldn't help but laugh at them. He realized there was something clever about the lies. Something smart.

Elvis was a pretty smart kid, he thought to himself. And they were brothers, he thought, too.

That *could* be neat —

Just then Elvis's eyes snapped open.

"Caught you!" said Elvis. He hadn't been asleep at all! "I never sleep."

Jesse jumped back, his heart pounding with surprise. He didn't say anything. He wasn't sure what to say. Instead he turned the flashlight off and rolled over on his back.

The kid is smart, all right, he thought as he tried to fall asleep. *Too* smart.

*   *   *

Jesse woke up just before dawn the next morning. This was the day he and Randolph were going to find Willy. He couldn't wait to wake up Glen and Annie and head out.

But the Greenwoods had other plans, Jesse discovered after poking his head inside their tent to wake them up. Like sleeping a little longer.

"Glen, it's seven in the morning," said Jesse. "C'mon. Let's go out on the boat with Randolph."

"You want to lower your voice?" begged Glen. "You'll wake up the bears."

"Don't you usually get up at noon?" asked Annie as she flopped over on her other side.

"Randolph leaves at dawn," said Jesse. "It's dawn."

"You go on ahead," said Glen. Then he rolled over to face Annie.

Jesse frowned and started to leave.

"Jess," he heard Annie call and stuck his head back inside the tent. "Take Elvis with you."

Jesse nearly choked. "No way!" he protested. But his protests fell on deaf ears. Minutes later he found himself walking toward the dock with Elvis following close behind.

"Hurry up," Jesse ordered his brother. Then he adjusted his baseball cap and picked up his step, making it tough for the younger boy to keep up.

"I'm walking as fast as I can," Elvis replied breathlessly.

"Try running."

"I can't help it if my legs are shorter than yours."

"If Randolph leaves without us, I'll kill you," Jesse threatened him.

"I have a black belt in karate."

"Yeah?" replied Jesse, unimpressed. "Well, I have laser death rays coming out of my eyes."

Elvis paused. "Liar," he said in disbelief.

A few minutes later thay had reached the dock. Jesse sighed with relief. Thankfully, *The Natselane* was still anchored. And Nadine was on deck, busy with some equipment.

Jesse raced ahead, leaving Elvis behind.

"Hi," he said to Nadine once he boarded the ship.

Nadine nodded politely, then turned away without saying a word.

Elvis climbed on board just in time to see Jesse's look of rejection. All he could do was stare at his older brother.

"What?" Jesse asked, feeling Elvis's eyes on him.

"Girls are the enemy," said Elvis.

"*You* are the enemy," said Jesse in frustration. Then he stormed off in search of Randolph.

"Cooties from the galaxy of Andromeda," Elvis shouted out after Jesse. "All girls have them."

Jesse found Randolph with some repairmen working on the engine. Something was wrong.

"I got a problem with the bilge pump," Randolph explained to Jesse with a heavy sigh.

"How big a problem?" asked Jesse. Dawn had come and gone and he wanted to see Willy again.

"It'll take me a couple of hours," replied Randolph. "Sorry."

Jesse fought back his disappointment. Then he noticed Nadine as she was leaving the ship and crossing into the woods.

"S'okay," he told Randolph. "See you in a couple of hours."

And with that Jesse headed back down the deck and pulled Elvis aside.

"Go back to the camp," he ordered Elvis. "Tell Glen and Annie I went out on the boat with Randolph, but you couldn't, because you get seasick."

"But that would be a lie," Elvis said.

"I think you can handle it," Jesse replied.

Chapter 13

Jesse made his way to a clearing. From there he could see an isolated little cove filled with driftwood, boulders, and slimy seaweed. The whole thing was surrounded on three sides by high rocky cliffs. The water was calm and tranquil and led out to the sea.

Nadine was sitting on the beach staring out at the water or the horizon, Jesse couldn't tell which. She seemed to him thoughtful and peaceful on the inside. Soft and beautiful on the outside.

He wanted so badly to go over and talk with her. But so far every time he had approached her, she had not seemed interested. Why? he wondered. What would he have to do to make her like him?

Jesse decided to wait and sat down behind a boulder. He watched her for some moments, waiting for some change in her mood that might give him the opportunity to go over.

Suddenly Nadine craned her neck forward. She had seen something in the water. Jesse looked, too. Swimming in the cove, almost close enough to touch, was a pod of orcas.

Jesse jumped to his feet, unable to help himself, and stood on the boulder. One of the orcas had a bent dorsal fin.

Just then Jesse slipped and slid off the boulders. He landed in the shallow depths of the cove, soaked from his backside to his feet.

Nadine swiveled around, now aware of Jesse's presence.

"What do you think you're doing?" she asked reproachfully.

Jesse smiled shyly. "I'm sitting in the ocean," he said, red-faced.

"You followed me, didn't you?" Nadine demanded to know.

Jesse shrugged. "So?" He had had it with

explaining himself to her. So he liked her. So what? And he showed it. What of it?

Something in his tone must have gotten through to Nadine because she held out her hand to help him up. Jesse took it and rose to his feet.

"What is this place?" he asked her.

"This is my favorite place on earth," she replied.

Jesse sat down in the spot where he had first seen Nadine sitting. He expected her to sit down beside him, but she didn't.

"I come here to be alone," she said, throwing a hint.

"We *are* alone," said Jesse in a take-charge tone of voice. He didn't care what Nadine thought of it. After a slight hesitation, she sat down next to Jesse.

"This is Rubbing Beach," she told him. "Orcas come from all over just to rub themselves on the bottom of the cove. Sometimes, if you sit here long enough, one of them will come really close."

"How close?"

"Ten feet once."

Jesse laughed. He could almost feel Willy's tongue on his fingertips. "You call that close?"

Nadine threw Jesse an admonishing stare. "These are wild orcas, not pets," she said sternly. "They're not amusement park rides. They don't like humans."

Jesse ignored Nadine's warning. Instead, he slowly pulled his harmonica out of his pocket and began to play it.

"Are you still trying to impress me?" Nadine asked him.

"Yeah," Jesse admitted between notes.

Nadine grimaced. She had to admit to herself that there was something likeable about Jesse. She recognized that from the start. But there was also something intangible. Something she couldn't put her finger on. And she didn't like that. She liked it when she could tell everything about someone the first time she met that person. Somehow it felt safer, as if she were the one who was in control. But Jesse was different. He seemed to keep a part of himself hidden and separate. Nadine didn't like it. Jesse made her uncomfortable.

Even Jesse's harmonica playing made her slightly ill at ease. The notes he played were haunting. They were sad notes. Lonely notes. Notes filled with a sense of loss. She wondered why Jesse played that way. She wondered if she would ever find out.

Just then her thoughts were interrupted as one of the whales popped out of the water and began swimming toward the beach. Jesse saw the whale, too, and scrambled down the rocks until he stood where the beach met the water. Once there he started playing his harmonica again. As if in answer to the notes the whale began to swim closer to the cove. Closer, Nadine noticed as she climbed down after Jesse, than any whale she had seen before. Soon it was close enough to touch.

Nadine watched as Jesse reached out and stroked the whale's round head. Or rather, she realized with astonishment, the whale *let* Jesse stroke its head. That's when she noticed that the whale had a bent dorsal fin. The sign of a whale who had spent time in captivity. She realized at once that the whale was Willy, the one Randolph had told her about many times.

"Open up," Jesse commanded Willy. "Let me give you a rubdown."

Jesse gave the signal, rolling his hand from side to side. Willy responded by opening his huge mouth wide, revealing all of his enormous sharp teeth, and sticking out his tongue. Jesse leaned over and stroked Willy's tongue several times. Nadine watched, awestruck.

All of a sudden something stirred in the water beside Willy. A second later a smaller orca broke through the water's surface. Jesse remembered Randolph describing the pod of whales the day before. This little one was Littlespot, Willy's younger brother.

Jesse reached his arm out hoping that Littlespot would open his mouth like Willy did. Instead, Littlespot ducked back under the water. Jesse laughed, realizing the younger orca was probably afraid to touch him.

Then Jesse heard someone else laugh. To his surprise, it was Nadine. He leaned in and began whispering into Willy's ear.

"Help me out here," he told the whale. "I want to introduce you to somebody." Then he gestured for Nadine to come closer to the cove.

Nadine hesitated. She had never been this close to a whale before.

"Willy, this is Nadine," said Jesse with a smile. "Nadine, Willy. Willy, give her a wave."

Jesse made another hand signal. This time Willy rolled onto his side, raised his flipper and slapped it onto the water.

Nadine smiled. In spite of her initial feelings toward Jesse, she was beginning to be impressed.

Jesse stroked Willy again. This time Willy shot an exuberant plume of water out of his blowhole, hitting the brim of Jesse's cap and sending it flying into the water.

"Hey, no fair!" Jesse said, laughing.

Jesse quickly removed his shirt and shoes and dove into the water after the hat. No sooner had he started swimming than Willy circled around him and nuzzled against him like a huge, overgrown kitten.

"Come on in," Jesse shouted to Nadine. "The water's fine."

"Jesse, get a grip," returned Nadine. "This is a killer whale."

Jesse laughed. "Naw," he said, giving Willy a gentle pat on the side. "He's a friend of mine."

Nadine watched in total wonder as Willy dived beneath the water and came up under

Jesse. Now Jesse was riding Willy as if the whale were a great sea horse. Together they circled the cove.

A few feet away Elvis was watching with wonder as well. He hadn't gone back to the campsite as Jesse ordered. Instead, he had followed Jesse, hiding behind some bushes so he wouldn't be seen. There was something about Jesse that fascinated him. Now, as he watched Jesse frolic around the water with the monstrous whale, Elvis couldn't help but admire him.

That's when he caught sight of Jesse's shirt lying askew against some rocks just a few inches from the water. The harmonica was jutting out of the shirt pocket. Maybe if he blew into the harmonica Willy would come to *him*, too, Elvis thought.

He carefully leaned forward and grabbed the harmonica. Then he took a deep breath. Just when he gave a good blow into the instrument something exploded up through the cove and drenched him with water.

It was Littlespot.

Up Littlespot came, chattering playfully at Elvis as he went. Littlespot wanted to play.

Elvis dropped the harmonica and his

heart skipped a beat. To him, Littlespot looked like a huge sea monster. He heard a terrified scream. Then he realized that it was he who was screaming. He turned on a dime and ran, terrified, back toward the campsite.

Chapter 14

Glen and Annie were sitting by the campfire husking corn when they were interrupted by the sound of running footsteps. They looked up just in time to see Elvis emerge from the woods. Out of breath, the boy just stood there as if he had something terribly important to tell them.

Glen and Annie just waited. Elvis was about to tell them about the whale that frightened him so, but then he would have to tell them how he stole Jesse's harmonica. He was sure they wouldn't approve of that. Still, by the look on their faces he knew that Glen and Annie were expecting him to say *something*. Finally, Elvis took a big swallow.

"I saw Jesse kissing Nadine!" he blurted out.

Glen and Annie looked at each other. They had known for some time that Jesse was becoming interested in some of the girls he had met in school. They also knew all along that it was only a matter of time before one of them, probably Glen, would have to sit down with Jesse and have a serious talk about the subject of dating girls.

It seemed to both of them that that time had just arrived.

Willy drew closer to the cove shore and let Jesse climb off him. Then he gracefully turned himself around and swam back out to sea where he joined the rest of his pod.

Jesse watched from the shore as the pod receded toward the horizon. He felt complete again, having been reunited with Willy. There had been something missing in his life since the first time he met Willy. Now he felt whole. It was a good feeling.

Nadine watched the pod, too. But she also found herself glancing back at Jesse.

She found she couldn't take her eyes off him. There was something more than ordinary about Jesse now. Something almost magical. She realized that Jesse was a very special kind of boy.

Jesse felt Nadine's eyes on him. "Maybe you can touch him next time," he told her.

"I can't believe he let you do that," said Nadine.

"I think he likes it."

Nadine nodded in agreement. They watched the pod of whales as they swam away. At the last moment Willy leaped up out of the water and dove, the last of the pod to disappear from view.

"Did you see that?" Nadine asked Jesse.

"Yeah," replied Jesse. But he wasn't looking at the whales. He was looking at her, admiring her beauty.

"You don't see that everyday."

"Nope," said Jesse, still looking at her.

Then Nadine turned away from the water and aimed her binoculars beyond the woods at the Greenwoods' campsite. She could see Elvis by the fire.

"He doesn't look anything like you," Nadine commented.

"Who?" asked Jesse. Then he looked at

the campsite himself. He could also see Elvis. His voice sank. "Yeah, well," he began to explain. "We have different dads."

Just then something at sea caught Jesse's eye. A hulking dark shape was crossing the water. It was so far away that at first Jesse thought it might have been a whale straying from Willy's pod. But when he took the binoculars from Nadine and looked through he saw that the dark shape was a ship. Its name, *The Dakar*, was painted across its side.

"What kind of a ship is that?" Jesse asked Nadine.

Nadine watched the ship. She recognized it even without binoculars.

"Oil tanker," she replied with distaste.

"Kind of ruins the view, doesn't it?" said Jesse.

"Tell me about it. They come through here like it's their own private highway."

Just then Glen emerged from the woods.

"Hey, Glen," said Jesse with surprise. "This is Nadine, Randolph's goddaughter."

"Hi," Glen said to Nadine. "Nice to meet you."

"Hi," replied Nadine.

"Jesse," said Glen. "Can I talk to you a second?"

Jesse nodded and followed Glen away from where Nadine sat. Jesse noticed that his foster father seemed somehow ill at ease and wondered why.

"Elvis saw you and Nadine," began Glen.

"Yeah?" replied Jesse. "That figures."

Glen looked at Jesse severely. Jesse could tell that there was something up and that it was serious.

"Listen," Glen began. "I was a lot like you when I was your age. But Annie's worried. She wanted me to talk to you about it. She thinks that kind of behavior can be dangerous."

It sounded as if Elvis told Glen all about Jesse riding on Willy's back.

"That's what Nadine thought, too," said Jesse. "But it's perfectly safe. I know exactly what I'm doing."

"I used to think that, too," said Glen, thinking back to when he started going out with girls.

"I'm practically an expert!" insisted Jesse.

Glen smiled. "I used to think *that*, too,"

he laughed. Then he put his arm on Jesse's shoulder and began speaking in a more serious tone of voice. "I know you're just going with your feelings," he told the boy earnestly. "You're a good kid. A smart kid. But it can lead to other things."

"Like what?" asked Jesse. He was beginning to get confused. How could playing with Willy lead to anything except fun?

"Well," Glen answered slowly. "Like sex."

Jesse's mouth practically dropped. "It can lead to sex? Glen, are you okay?"

"I'm fine. Why?"

"Because I don't know what you're talking about."

"I'm talking about you kissing Nadine."

"Who said anything about kissing Nadine?"

Glen and Jesse stared at each other for a long moment as the same answer came to their minds: Elvis.

Glen wasted no time in returning to the campsite. He couldn't remember when he had felt more humiliated. So far on this trip Elvis had done nothing but make up lies and cause trouble. All right, thought Glen. Maybe the kid is looking for attention. If

it was attention he wanted, it would be attention he would get.

When he got back to the campsite, it was just in time to stop Elvis from sipping his cocoa. He led Elvis to the small tent. Then he placed him inside.

"You're not going anywhere," he told Elvis angrily.

"But I'm hungry," insisted Elvis.

"So eat your hat," Glen answered back. Then he closed the flaps and zipped the tent up tight.

At that moment he was so angry, he considered never opening it up again.

Chapter 15

The next morning Jesse and Nadine went back to the cove in the hopes of seeing J-pod again. They both wore bathing suits. This time Nadine was going to go into the water, too.

They sat on the rocks that overlooked the cove and waited. At first the sky was orange from the rising sun, but it soon turned into a bright, clear blue.

While they waited they talked. Now Nadine wanted to know everything about Jesse. She had known only a little about him, Randolph having once told her something of how he and Jesse freed Willy from the seaquarium two years earlier.

But Nadine knew there was more. There was a mysterious side of Jesse that she wanted to know more about. So she asked questions and listened intently as Jesse told her about his early days as a runaway from the juvenile center and how he used to live from foster home to foster home. Then he told her about how he was finally placed with the Greenwoods and how, at first, he couldn't trust them. Or *wouldn't* trust them.

Then he met Willy. To his surprise he was the only human the whale seemed to trust. He reasoned that was because he himself had been in a kind of captivity. He himself knew what it was like to be lonely and without a family.

Soon he felt he understood Willy better than anybody else. By that time he knew that unless Willy was set free and reunited with his own family, he would die.

He had saved Willy's life.

After listening to Jesse's story, Nadine now understood Jesse's relationship with the huge, friendly orca. She looked out at the cove longing to see Willy again. Where yesterday she had been frightened by the mammoth creature, she now felt curious.

Now she, like Jesse, wanted to touch Willy, to pet him. To be close to him.

Just then her heart skipped a beat when she saw some movement out on the water. It was J-pod. After a moment one whale broke away from the pod and began making his way toward the cove. It was Willy.

Jesse rose excitedly to his feet and dove into the water. Then Nadine, somewhat more hesitantly, followed.

Once underwater, Nadine trailed Jesse as he swam toward the whale. Nadine had been underwater before, but never this close to such a graceful, but huge, creature. Everything seemed to move in slow motion as she and Jesse followed the whale to the bottom of the cove.

At the bottom Willy rubbed himself against the smooth rocks of the cove's floor as if he had an itch he was trying to scratch. Jesse and Nadine playfully imitated him and touched the bottom, too. Then, as Willy began to rise toward the water's surface, they followed.

The kids broke through the surface, taking big gasps of air as they did. While they swam, Elvis was standing on the shore

blowing haphazardly into Jesse's harmonica.

Jesse figured that Glen had finally re-
leased Elvis from solitary confinement.
Then Elvis must have swiped Jesse's harmonica. Now Elvis was crouching on the
beach playing to the other whales in the J-
pod. Littlespot broke away from the group
and swam over. When Littlespot got close
enough, Elvis pointed a water gun at the
whale and squirted him. Littlespot responded giddily and squirted Elvis back,
spraying the boy from his blowhole. Elvis
fell onto the ground laughing joyously.

Then Elvis sprayed Littlespot again with
a blast from his water gun. Littlespot responded by spitting water at him.

In the meantime, Jesse and Nadine followed Willy to the bottom of the cove. This
time Willy nudged at Nadine gently. Nadine was taken aback, uncertain what to
do. She even became a little frightened and
reached out to grab hold of Jesse's hand.

Sensing Nadine's uneasiness, Jesse led
her up to the surface. Once there they could
hear the sound of whalesong coming from
further out at sea. It was Willy's mother

calling him and Littlespot to return to the pod.

In a matter of moments the two whales heard Catspaw's calls and began swimming away from the cove. Soon they drifted off with the rest of their family.

Elvis, watching from the shore, was sad when Littlespot turned away and swam off.

"We'll meet again, Fish!" he called out to the whale, almost as if it were a challenge. Then he looked around for Jesse and Nadine. Just a moment ago he had seen them climb out of the water and walk along the beach. But where were they now?

Then he saw them further down the beach.

Nadine and Jesse looked into each other's eyes, oblivious to Elvis, who was just a few feet away.

Nadine slowly leaned forward and kissed Jesse on the lips. It was a short, gentle kiss.

Jesse felt his emotions swell. He wasn't sure what the kiss meant. Nor did he care. For now all he knew was that he cared strongly for Nadine. More strongly than for any girl he had ever known in his life.

Chapter 16

That night a strong wind blew across the sea. The waters that ran from Rubbing Beach to the ocean became choppy. Overhead, thunder rumbled and lightning ripped across the sky. A torrent of rain began to fall.

Aboard *The Dakar* Captain Nilson cursed as he checked his depth finder and compass. Visibility was low. The currents were making the waters hard to navigate. He was already behind schedule, but now he knew he would have to slow down. To make matters worse, Nilson realized, engine pressure was dropping at an alarming rate.

"We're losing engine pressure!" Nilson shouted into the intercom. "I won't be able to hold course in these currents!"

Nilson's voice could barely be heard several levels below in the engine room. Down there, danger alarms blared and steam valves hissed, creating a deafening din.

Then there was an explosion of steam and brass. The force of the explosion threw one engineer across the room. Exploding steam burned another across the face, nearly blinding him.

"What is it?" a frantic engineer shouted out from the back of the room. He couldn't see through the blasting steam.

The lights began to flicker, the whole room went black, and the intercom went dead.

The Dakar was helpless at sea. On the bridge Captain Nilson cursed again as he felt the power leave his great ship like a living thing that had just drawn its last breath. Now the ship was drifting and he was powerless to control its course.

That's when he noticed something through the viewing window that made his heart skip a beat. A flashing buoy marked a one-way controlled traffic area. That meant they were closer to shallow waters than Nilson had realized. With no power and no light few ships could survive without crashing into the many coral reefs that jutted out of the beaches in the area.

Unable to warn his crew, he held on to the control panel and braced himself for the worst.

Jesse lay awake in his sleeping bag listening to the gale winds as they blew against the outside of his tent.

He was thinking about the events of that afternoon and couldn't sleep. First he thought about Willy and the other whales. Willy seemed so different than he had two years before. The great whale seemed at peace and Jesse assumed that it had something to do with being reunited with his family.

Then he thought of Nadine. They had made a special connection that afternoon. It was, for Jesse, at once a new sensation and a familiar one. Nadine was different than any girl he had ever met at school, yet it was as if she had awakened a part of him that had always been there, inside. Thinking of Nadine made him feel calm and peaceful and good about himself.

Then thoughts of Elvis crept into his mind. But, somehow, the thoughts didn't make him gag as they had in the past. The image of Elvis playing with Littlespot along the cove reminded him too much of how he must have looked the first time Randolph saw him play with Willy at Northwest Adventure Park.

Jesse looked over at Elvis. Asleep, Elvis looked angelic. At that moment he didn't look like the boy that Jesse had come to know as a compulsive liar. Jesse realized that Elvis used lies as protection against the outside world. There must be something behind those lies, he thought. Something too hard for Elvis to face.

That's when he realized that he could just as well have been thinking about himself. It was something he had been feeling, but kept pushing to the back of his mind. Yet every time he looked at Elvis he was reminded of it. That had made him resent Elvis even more.

Suddenly he found he couldn't suppress his thoughts anymore. There were some questions he needed the answers to and only Elvis had them.

He turned on his flashlight, leaned over and aimed it into Elvis's face.

"Are you awake?" he asked.

Elvis stirred and squinted in the bright light. "Yeah," he said.

"I have to ask you something."

"Okay."

Jesse paused. He wanted to ask the question just right, while it was still fresh in his mind.

"Did Mom ever talk about me? About before you were born?" he asked. "When she lived out here?"

Elvis's eyes suddenly went limp, as if try as he might he couldn't brush away Jesse's question with a lie.

"No," he said flatly. Jesse knew he was telling the truth.

"Did she ever talk about my dad?" Jesse asked.

"No."

"Did she ever talk about me?"

Elvis paused. "No," he finally said.

Jesse looked away. "Oh," he said, unable to hide his disappointment.

"She had problems," said Elvis.

Jesse looked up, somewhat startled at his brother's candid remark.

"Yeah? Like what?" he asked.

"She lied all the time," Elvis sighed. "She said she loved me."

"Maybe she did, Elvis," said Jesse.

"She said she would never leave," Elvis said.

Jesse looked at Elvis. The pain in his brother's eyes cut through Jesse like a knife.

J-pod watched the hulking *Dakar* as it moved toward a landing further up on the beach. They had migrated a few hundred yards from the cove at Rubbing Beach looking for the relative safety of shallower waters until the worst of the storm had passed. But now they sensed that a new danger was growing near.

It was Willy who first sensed the danger. When he sensed *The Dakar* approach, he let out a low squeal that warned the other whales of the danger. Soon Catspaw, Luna, Littlespot, and the rest of the pod began to stir with similar squeals, each whale trying to warn the others.

The whales scurried to move out of the

cove. Some made it back out to sea, but *The Dakar* was approaching quickly, drifting on the incoming waves.

One of the whales that made it to safety was Catspaw. No sooner had she reached deeper waters than she realized her three children were nowhere to be seen. She called out to them, but no one answered.

They were still in the cove.

In the meantime *The Dakar* closed in on the landing, its huge form eventually creating a partial barricade between the whales and the sea. Willy, Luna, and Littlespot tried desperately to find a way around the ship, but there was no room. Now the ship was slicing closer, like some huge dark knife.

The whales panicked. They circled and scattered, but soon felt themselves pushed further back toward shallower waters and the beach.

Then it happened. *The Dakar*'s bow struck some jagged rocks. A horrible loud sound, that of metal scraping against metal, deafened Willy and the other whales as the ship's hull began to crack against the rocks.

Soon *The Dakar* had come to a helpless

stop and became embedded in the sands of the shoal. But by then the hull of *The Dakar* had split open and a thick black liquid began to pour out. The crude oil. It emptied generously into the waters, blackening everything in sight with its thickness. Soon the oil began to drift downward along the beach and toward the cove at Rubbing Beach.

The whales were jarred by the rippling effect as the ship crashed through the water. Willy and Littlespot were tossed in one direction, Luna in another.

When Willy and Littlespot recovered they found themselves near a section of the cove that led safely out to sea. Both whales could hear their mother calling to them from the distance. They were about to follow the call to safety when they noticed that Luna wasn't with them.

They dove below the surface and searched the water with their eyes. Finally they saw Luna at the far end, near where *The Dakar* had run aground. She, too, had heard Catspaw's calls and was searching for her, trying to swim in her direction.

Luna swam hard, desperate to be reunited with her mother. But soon the water became thick and heavy and took on a foul, thick stench. After a while she could no longer make out the eddies of the water. Everything was pitch-black.

She had entered an oil slick.

Suddenly the thick black oil began to seep into Luna's spout and nostrils. It became difficult for her to breath. She struggled to reach the surface of the water. The weight of the heavy oil slowed her down. Finally she broke through the surface, but by this time all her strength was gone. She drifted slowly toward the shore of the cove, coming to a stop only when she, like *The Dakar*, had become trapped in the sand.

Chapter 17

At dawn Jesse was awakened by faint whis-
pers that traveled on the breeze. At first
he thought he was dreaming, but soon he
realized that this was real.

He was hearing the mournful sounds of
orcas crying. The whales were in trouble.

Jesse jumped out of his sleeping bag,
slipped on his shoes and jacket, and hurried
through the woods. He was halfway to the
cove when he heard footsteps. Someone
was following him. He pressed himself
against a tree and waited to see who it was.

Seconds later he saw Elvis winding
through the woods, cursing each time he

caught his clothes on a branch. Somehow Jesse was not surprised.

Jesse jumped out from behind the tree. His first instinct was to boot Elvis back to the campsite, but the despondent sounds of the whales could be heard louder now.

"Come on," Jesse said, turning back into the woods. As they went, the whale cries became louder. "There. Hear that?" Jesse asked Elvis.

"What is it?" asked Elvis.

"Orcas."

"Yeah," said Elvis. "Sad ones."

The two boys raced forward. It wasn't long before they reached the clearing that led to the cove. From the clearing they could see Littlespot spyhopping in the shallow waters of Rubbing Beach. Each time the whale jumped he let out a desperate cry. A few feet away from Littlespot, Willy was circling in the water. Jesse became scared. Both whales were acting lost and confused. Something was terribly wrong, but he couldn't tell what it was.

That's when he and Elvis noticed another whale lying on the beach, half out of the water.

It was Luna. She was listlessly moving her head from side to side as if she were too weak to lift it completely. As they got closer Jesse could hear that she was having trouble breathing as well. Luna was sick.

Jesse and Elvis climbed down the rocks and raced to the beach. They moved carefully toward Luna, uncertain what she might do if they approached. But Luna was clearly too weak to move. She just lay there, helpless.

As they approached her Jesse noticed the strange-looking substance that was covering Luna's skin. He reached out and ran his hand along her head.

Suddenly Jesse felt scared. Luna wasn't just sick. She was covered in oil. Oil that was dripping from her eyelids, down the side of her face and out of her mouth. It had even filled her spout.

But it was worse than that. Jesse soon realized that not only was Luna covered with oil, but the water around her was darkened with it as well. And it was spreading.

"Wake up!" shouted Elvis as he burst into Glen and Annie's tent. Then he began to shake Glen awake. "There's been a terrible accident! Some kind of oil spill in the ocean trapped some whales! Willy's sister is beached and she's sick real bad! You have to call Randolph! I think maybe a ship crashed or something! It's a major disaster!"

Glen and Annie glanced at each other and rolled their eyes. By now they were too used to Elvis's exaggerated claims.

"Go back to sleep," Glen told Elvis.

"But I'm telling the truth!" insisted Elvis. How could he convince them, he wondered? How could he make them believe that he and Jesse had discovered Luna beached on the shore of the cove? That she was covered from end to end with oil? That Jesse had told him to run back and tell Glen and Annie to find Randolph?

He didn't have to. At that moment Luna's plaintive cries reached Glen and Annie's ears.

"I'll call Randolph," said Glen as he and Annie feverishly began to get dressed.

Less than an hour later everyone had converged on the cove. Randolph had begun to apply some gauze to Luna's blowhole and was saturating it with fluid. Then he put a sample into a plastic bag and handed it to Nadine.

"Run this down to the lab," he told Nadine. "Tell them it's from me and it's an emergency."

Nadine took off, sample bag in hand.

Randolph turned to the others. "Let's go," he said. Jesse, Glen, and Annie closed in on Luna. Together with Randolph they began to rock the small whale back and forth in an effort to slide her back into the water.

Elvis wanted to help, but was too small. He stood on the shore and watched as Jesse and the others finally got Luna into the water.

But even in the water Luna was too weak to swim. She just floated there, bobbing up and down, wheezing instead of breathing.

"She needs help, Randolph," said Jesse.

"The institute is bringing in Kate Haley, our vet from the mainland," Randolph informed Jesse.

Willy began to swim slow circles around his sister spraying her with water each time he went by.

"Way to go, Willy!" Jesse called out. "You saved your sis — "

But Willy ignored Jesse and swam away.

Jesse looked helplessly at Randolph. "What's the matter with him?" he asked.

"His sister is dying," explained Randolph.

"But we're all on the same side, aren't we?" asked Jesse. It seemed to him that Willy was guarding Luna as he circled around her. As if he was protecting her from something. Something horrible.

Jesse shuddered as he wondered what it was.

Chapter 18

John Milner sat in the backseat of one of Benbrook Oil Company's private cars and cursed as he watched the evening news on a portable television set.

"The Dakar," said the local news reporter who was standing in front of the beached oil tanker, "a forty-year-old Liberian oil tanker, ran aground on Lawson's Reef at 12:05 last night, spilling thousands of gallons of raw crude into the water, endangering fish and other wildlife indigenous to this region."

Milner had just gotten off the phone with Alexander Benbrook, Jr., owner of the oil company. Benbrook was concerned. It was Milner who had personally overseen the shipment of crude that *The Dakar* was delivering. Now it was he who had to explain what happened. Milner had no explanation. He had passed the details of the shipment down the pike to a committee. It was the committee who hired the ship that was delivering the crude. In the end, however, he knew that the responsibility was his. And it was he who would have to answer to Mr. Benbrook for the accident.

Milner quickly changed the channel.

" — and in a related story," another local newscaster said as the program broadcast a shot of the cove, "three young orcas have taken refuge from the spill in a small cove near Bright's Landing. A team of experts is assembling to see what, if anything, can be done for them."

A paper inched out of a fax machine on a console on the far side of the car. Milner's assistant read it and handed it to his boss, but Milner brushed it aside.

"Just tell me what I want to know," he ordered the assistant. "Tell me we chartered two tug escorts."

"No," the assistant replied, his voice etched with grave concern.

"Tell me the ship was up to code," he said.

"Legally, the ship was up to code," said the assistant. "We were completely within the law. But — "

"But what?"

"But *The Dakar*'s a cheap piece of tin. We always knew that."

Milner threw the assistant a look of near-animal venom. Heads would roll, he promised himself. He hit his remote and turned the TV channel again.

"The single-hull tanker," yet another local newscaster reported as pictures of *The Dakar* flashed across the screen, "which is under the payroll of the Benbrook Oil Company, was built well before 1990, the year when double hulls became mandatory for all new vessels. And our sources indicate that Benbrook, as a matter of policy, has chosen not to retrofit its pre-1990 fleet with the double innerlinings that many feel could go a long way to prevent disasters like this one."

Milner felt something sink in the pit of

his stomach. He didn't know how he was going to do it, but he had to turn this disaster around so that Benbrook Oil's reputation wouldn't be destroyed. He immediately began to think of his options.

Dr. Kate Haley watched from the passenger seat of the seaplane as it approached the cove. The scene below was mayhem. Reporters were everywhere. The beach was cordoned off by police. The Coast Guard had set up camp in a nearby amphitheatre.

In the center of everything were the whales. Luna, Haley could see, was the worst off. She seemed the weakest as she bobbed up and down on the waves of the shallow water. The other two seemed as if they would have a better chance for survival.

When the seaplane landed, Haley climbed out and was greeted by Blake, the Coast Guard commander.

"I'm Kate Haley," she said, introducing herself.

Blake had heard of Dr. Haley. She was the best vet the Orca Institute had. "Commander Blake, Coastal Marine Patrol," he said, extending his hand. "Most of your medical team is already here."

Indeed, as soon as Dr. Haley was led to the amphitheatre, a score of Orca Institute vets converged on her. One of them handed her a clipboard and chart and apprised her of the situation.

"Kate." She heard a familiar voice call her name. She looked up. Randolph was making his way toward her through the crowd. Jesse was by his side.

"Randolph!" she exclaimed happily.

"I'm glad you're here," said Randolph as he reached her.

"Me, too," nodded Dr. Haley. Then she looked at the notes on her clipboard. "How long ago was the culture taken?"

"Three hours," said Randolph, referring to the sample he had taken from Luna and had Nadine bring to the lab.

"Let's do this now," began Dr. Haley. "Before she gets any worse."

"You a doctor?" asked Jesse, trying to be noticed.

"Jesse's the one who found them," Randolph explained to Dr. Haley.

"Jesse?" asked Dr. Haley. The name

rang familiar to her. "Randolph's told me all about you. I'm going to do my best, Jesse," Dr. Haley promised sincerely.

"The boat's ready, Kate," a vet called from beyond the crowd. Dr. Haley started to go, but noticed Jesse's worried expression.

"Hey, don't worry," she said, winking at him. "I'm really good at this." Then she walked off through the crowd.

"Willy doesn't like doctors," Jesse reminded Randolph.

"She's one of the good ones, Jess."

Jesse watched as Dr. Haley disappeared among the other vets. "But Willy doesn't know that," he said warily.

Just then Jesse saw a television news crew besiege Dr. Haley and her team as they headed for the cove shore.

"Dr. Haley," began the reporter. "What are the whales' chances for survival?"

Dr. Haley showed a sign of irritation as she faced the cameras.

"These orcas have been exposed to highly toxic unrefined crude oil," Dr. Haley explained. Jesse listened carefully. Until now he had known that the whales were in trouble, but he hadn't known why. Dr.

Haley continued: "From a mile away you can hear they're having trouble breathing. Tests of the female orca show signs of severe respiratory infection. So, if you'll excuse me, I've got to get to work if I'm going to give your story a happy ending."

Then Dr. Haley pushed past the cameras and led her team to the shore where a small outboard motorboat was waiting to take them to Luna.

For the moment, Jesse felt better. Dr. Haley had handled the reporters quickly and efficiently. Then she pushed them out of the way so she could help the whales. That meant that she really cared about them.

Jesse went to the top of the rocks for a better view. Nadine, Glen, Annie, and Elvis were already there. From that point on the rocks everyone could see the cove, where the whales were trapped.

Now Jesse got his first look at the danger of the situation.

Jesse knew that if Dr. Haley and her team didn't help Luna fast, the young female whale would soon be trapped in the cove. He also knew that Willy would never leave his sister and Littlespot would do whatever Willy did.

If that happened, Jesse realized, Catspaw would lose her family.

And he would lose Willy forever.

Chapter 19

Jesse watched through a pair of binoculars as Dr. Haley and the other vets slowed their motorboat and approached Luna. He could see that one of the vets had opened up a medical case and had started to pull out some equipment. That's when he saw the hypodermic needle.

"Oh, no," he gasped.

"What?" Glen wanted to know.

"They're going to inject Luna with a needle bigger than my arm."

Glen knew what Jesse was thinking. Two years ago, when he was really sick, Willy had reacted violently to the sight of a vet's needle.

"Maybe he doesn't remember the doctors at the seaquarium," Glen said as they shared a concerned look.

Jesse nodded cautiously in agreement, but he wasn't convinced. He turned his sights back toward the water. The motorboat had come to a full stop right next to Luna. One of the vets had just finished filling the huge hypo with serum.

Just then, Willy caught sight of the needle and began inching his way toward Luna. Dr. Haley and the vets hesitated. Jesse knew they were waiting to see if Willy was going to let them inject Luna.

Then Willy submerged and was gone. The vets sighed. Dr. Haley took the hypo and aimed it at a spot on Luna's oil-covered skin.

Suddenly the motorboat shook and the water around it rippled. Willy had come up right behind it and began pushing it away from Luna and back toward the shore. He pushed and pushed until the boat was closer to the shore than it was to Luna.

Finally Willy stopped pushing the boat. But instead of swimming away he lingered near the boat for a moment, his huge eye defiantly focused at Dr. Haley.

Jesse was taken aback. He had never seen Willy act quite like that before. It was as if the huge whale was issuing a warning to Dr. Haley. A warning telling her not to hurt Luna.

For the first time since he could remember, Jesse was frightened by Willy.

Later that evening Jesse, Elvis, and the Greenwoods had just returned to their campsite when a car pulled up. Randolph, Dr. Haley, and John Milner got out. Randolph told Jesse that they needed his help if they were going to save Luna, but it was Milner who began explaining to Jesse just how.

Jesse didn't like the oil company representative. After all, it was Benbrook Oil's fault that *The Dakar* crashed, anyway. And it was their fault that the whales were in danger. No, he decided. He didn't trust Milner at all.

But Randolph had asked Jesse to hear Milner out. Yes, Milner was probably out for his own interests, but the fact remained that without Jesse's help Luna might die. Willy was too protective of his little sister to let Dr. Haley administer the needed antibiotic to her. And Jesse was the only one who could get through to Willy.

"I'm not going to lie to you, Jesse," said Milner. Jesse looked around the campsite. "This is an awful situation and my company is to blame for it. It's very important to me that no harm comes to these whales. And that, according to your friend Randolph, is where you come in."

"I won't allow you to put him in danger," Annie warned Milner.

"He's just a kid," added Glen.

Dr. Haley touched Annie's arm. "I won't allow him to be put in danger, either," she said reassuringly. "It will be all right. But we need him."

"I could help out, too," said Elvis excitedly. "Littlespot likes me. I could — "

But Glen raised his finger to his lips, cutting Elvis off.

Milner continued to look Jesse in the eyes. "Willy trusts you, Jesse," he began.

"And he doesn't trust you," Jesse shot back.

"He thinks he's protecting Luna," Dr. Haley interrupted. "But in fact he's keeping us from her. He's killing her. You're his only friend. You can help him. You can save Luna."

Jesse thought about it. He knew from the start that Willy was going to be a problem if Luna was to be saved. He also knew that he was probably the only person who could persuade Willy to let the vets help Luna.

"I'll make a deal with you," said Jesse.

"I'm listening," replied Milner with a smile. Deal making was something he understood.

"I'll convince Willy to let us help Luna," Jesse offered.

"Great," said Milner and he waited for Jesse's conditions.

"But you have to promise to get Willy, Luna, and Littlespot back to their mother."

Milner hesitated. He knew he might not be able to keep the promise if he made it.

"I'm not God, Jesse," he said. "I don't know if the whales will get better. And there are a lot of people to answer to, here. I can't promise that."

"Fine," said Jesse firmly. "But it's your oil that's killing Luna, and if she dies, everybody's going to see it on the six

124

o'clock news. And everybody's going to blame you. Just promise me you'll try."

Milner thought for a second. Realizing he had nothing to lose, he held out his hand. "I promise," he said.

"There is one thing I'm gonna need," Jesse told Milner after shaking his hand.

"You name it," said Milner.

Jesse stood up and smiled. "Chocolate."

Chapter 20

The next morning Elvis sat on the rocks that overlooked the cove at Rubbing Beach, looking sadly at the dock below. Jesse was standing on the dock staring out at the cove at Willy and Littlespot, who were still circling Luna as they had been for the last two days. Further down the shore Dr. Haley and her medical team were loading up a small motorboat with supplies.

"Mind if I join you?" came a voice from behind Elvis. He didn't have to look to know it was Annie.

"You can do whatever you want," he said uninvitingly. "I'm just a guest, remember?"

Annie sat down next to Elvis. She hesitated before saying anything. She knew how sensitive he could be and wanted to phrase her questions just right.

Finally she asked: "You gonna tell me what's bothering you?"

"Nothing."

"You and Jesse seem to be getting along pretty good now."

"I hate him," Elvis said sharply.

Annie was surprised at how harsh Elvis sounded. "I know that's not true," she said.

"Yes it is," insisted Elvis. Then he turned around to face Annie. By the puffiness around his eyes it was clear he had been crying.

"He's your brother, Elvis," Annie said, concerned. Elvis turned away again.

"The whole world kisses Jesse's butt," he said. "I'm tired of it."

"Elvis, this family doesn't kiss butts. We don't play favorites."

Elvis turned around again. This time he was smiling. "I want to help," he said eagerly.

"The whales need all the help they can get," said Annie, eyeing him skeptically. Had Elvis been crying crocodile tears just to get what he wanted? she wondered. "Everybody has to pitch in."

"You promise I can help?" Elvis asked, now even more eagerly.

"I promise."

"Will you spit and shake on it?" Elvis spit into his hand and held it out. Annie gulped, grossed out, and did the same. Then they clasped hands.

Elvis turned and looked down at the cove. Then he turned back to Annie and nodded and followed her down off the rocks.

By the time Elvis and Annie reached the dock, Randolph and Glen had arrived. Jesse had grabbed a large plastic trash bag from a pile of supplies and was now starting to climb off the dock and into a small rubber raft.

Elvis looked up at Annie then called out: "Jesse?"

"Yeah?" replied Jesse as he balanced himself on the raft.

"Good luck," Elvis said after a short pause.

Taken aback, Jesse looked at Elvis. "Thanks," he said. Then he settled himself into the raft and glanced over at the medical team's motorboat just in time to see Dr. Haley preparing the large syringe for Luna.

"You better not let Willy see that," he told Dr. Haley.

"Tell me about it," Dr. Haley agreed. "You ready?"

"No," Jesse said with an anxious sigh.

"Good," smiled Dr. Haley. "Me, neither."

Jesse picked up two oars and pushed off in the raft. Dr. Haley and her team followed. When Jesse reached the square, wooden diving platform at the mouth of the cove, he stopped the raft. Then he climbed on to the platform, taking the big plastic bag with him.

Jesse looked back at the pier. By now a crowd of onlookers and reporters had gathered. Then he looked out to the water. Willy and Littlespot continued to circle Luna diligently.

Jesse took his harmonica out of his pocket and began to play. The notes were sweet and melodic, the ones he knew Willy used to respond to. But this time Willy ignored the music, choosing instead to stay by Luna's side.

Just then the crowd on the shore began to murmur with excitement. Jesse noticed that Willy began swimming faster, agitated by the noise. Then Willy bumped the raft.

"You have to get rid of those jerks," Jesse told Dr. Haley as he pointed to the shore. "They're upsetting him."

Dr. Haley nodded to Commander Blake on the pier. Soon the Coast Guard began to disperse the crowd. When the shore was cleared, Jesse turned back to Willy and began playing his harmonica again. This time he played slower and more soulfully, almost as if he were begging the huge whale to approach him.

At last, Willy broke away from his sister and floated toward Jesse. Littlespot even followed. Jesse smiled. Now it was like old times. But Willy stopped short of the platform and stared at Jesse. Willy's stare made him uncomfortable. It didn't look friendly.

Then Willy nudged the platform gently with his snout, then nudged it again only harder. Jesse felt the platform rock. Suddenly a realization hit him: Willy was trying to scare him off.

The thought bothered Jesse. Somehow

Willy didn't trust him anymore. That was not what Jesse wanted.

"I'm not going to hurt you," he said to the whale. "I want to help."

But Willy wasn't listening. Instead he let out an angry screech and rammed into the platform even harder. This time Jesse was nearly thrown off the platform.

"Come on, Willy," pleaded Jesse. "Luna needs us. We can save her. Please!"

Then Jesse remembered the plastic bag he brought from the pier and opened it up. The bag was filled with small salmon, just as he had requested from Milner. He pulled one out and waved it before Willy's eyes.

"How about some chocolate, Willy?" Jesse asked. "For old time's sake, huh?"

Willy eyed the salmon hesitantly.

"I know you probably eat live ones now," Jesse continued, trying to keep his voice even and friendly. "But it's the best I could do. What do you say? Let me help you get back to your mom. Please . . ."

Finally, Willy slowly opened his mouth. Jesse smiled. Then he leaned over and carefully placed the salmon on Willy's tongue. Willy swallowed it and happily shot a plume of water from his spout.

"That-a-boy!" Jesse exclaimed. Willy trusted him again. "I promise I won't let you down." Then he turned to Dr. Haley and nodded. "It's okay," he told her.

One of the vets revved up the motor in Dr. Haley's boat and began driving it toward Luna.

"This is Dr. Haley," Jesse told Willy as the motorboat crossed by the platform. "She's going to help Luna."

"Hi, Willy," Dr. Haley said cautiously as she passed the whale. "We already met."

After a few moments the motorboat pulled up alongside Luna.

"It's going to be okay, Luna," Jesse could hear Dr. Haley say to the young whale. Her voice was soft and sweet, just like a doctor talking to a patient. "Ooh, you don't sound so good." Then Dr. Haley called out to Jesse: "We need to get her to raise her fluke."

Jesse nodded and turned to Willy. "You have to show Luna what to do," he told Willy. "If you do it, she will."

Jesse raised his arm. It was the old signal for Willy to raise his fluke. But Willy didn't move. Jesse tried again. This time Willy obeyed.

As soon as she saw Willy raise his fluke Luna struggled to do the same. Her movements were slow and labored, but finally she managed to lift hers as well.

"That's good, Luna," Dr. Haley whispered. "That's really good." Then she pulled out the syringe, prepped it once or twice, and gave Luna the shot.

Jesse watched from the platform. "Thanks, Willy," he said as he stroked the whale. "You just saved your sister's life."

A little while later Jesse and Dr. Haley returned to the shore and went to the communications tent. They were greeted by John Milner and Randolph.

"You hit it out of the park, kid," Milner said to Jesse. "I'm impressed."

Jesse eyed Milner suspiciously. There was still something about the oil company executive he didn't trust.

"All we can do now is wait and see how she responds," said Dr. Haley. "You did good work, Jesse."

"I was scared," Jesse admitted, although he knew it showed.

"Well," began Dr. Haley, "when you've been doing this for as long as I have, I promise you, you'll be twice as scared."

Jesse forced a laugh. That's when he noticed that Randolph hadn't said a word since he and Dr. Haley returned to shore. And from the expression on Randolph's face Jesse could tell something was wrong.

"What's the matter?" Jesse asked Randolph.

Randolph walked over to the wall and pointed at a spot on a mounted map. "The oil slick is being pulled by currents right toward the cove," he said gravely. "We don't have much time."

Chapter 21

Just before dusk Jesse went down to the pier and stood on the dock. Willy's sister was sick and Willy was very protective of her. But what if Dr. Haley and the others couldn't save Luna? How would Willy feel toward Jesse then? He remembered how easy it had once been between him and Willy and wondered if it would ever be like that again.

After a while Jesse heard someone approach him. He turned around. It was Nadine. She sat down next to him and dangled her legs over the side of the dock, too.

"Their mom is probably going crazy from

worrying," Nadine said as she watched the whales.

"Luna's going to get better," Jesse said hopefully. "I know it. It's all going to be okay."

Nadine looked away. Her eyes saddened.

"What?" asked Jesse, sensing something was wrong.

"No matter what, Jesse," she said. "It's not *all* going to be okay. It's all *ruined*. This is just your summer vacation. You can go home. But this is my backyard."

Nadine began to cry. Jesse reached into his coat pocket, but couldn't find a tissue. So he pulled his pocket inside out and ripped it off.

"Here," he said, handing her the torn pocket.

Nadine looked quizzically at the pocket.

"I don't have a Kleenex," Jesse explained. "It's the best I can do."

Nadine couldn't help but laugh through her tears. She took the pocket and blew her nose into it. When she was done she and Jesse stared at each other for a long moment.

"You want your pocket back?" Nadine asked.

"No, that's okay," Jesse said gently and wiped a remaining tear from her cheek.

Jesse saw Nadine back to *The Natselane*, then returned to his campsite. The Greenwoods had turned in early and a few remaining embers of the campfire were still flickering.

Jesse went into his tent, his body aching with exhaustion. Elvis was already in his sleeping bag, but he was awake and looking at something he was holding in his hands. It was the orca necklace Randolph had given Jesse.

"Who said you could touch that?" Jesse asked accusingly.

"The President of the United States," replied Elvis in his usual smart-alecky way. "He announced it on TV. Where were you?"

Jesse let it go, surprising himself. He realized how used to Elvis he had become by now.

"It's pretty cool, huh?" he said as he climbed into his sleeping bag.

Elvis turned the wooden orca over in his hand, fascinated by it. "Yeah," he said, "What's it for?"

"You really want to know?"

137

"Not if it's a long story," Elvis replied.

Jesse smiled. "There was this young Haida Indian named Natselane," Jesse began. Elvis's eyes immediately became riveted to him. "He lived many years ago, before there were whales. One day Natselane got lost and couldn't find his way home. He carved the first ever whale out of a log . . ."

"Come on," Elvis interrupted snidely. "A big wooden fish?"

"You want to hear this story or not?"

"I bet the whale comes to life," said Elvis.

"That's right," replied Jesse.

"I bet he gets back to his family, too."

The two became silent for a moment. The word "family" echoed in their thoughts and lingered between them like an invisible cord.

"Natselane prayed so hard to get back to his family," Jesse continued softly, "that the whale came to life. And Natselane rode on the back of the whale all the way home."

Again the boys fell silent. Elvis looked away and Jesse could tell he must be thinking about their mother and the life he must have had with her. Up until now, Jesse realized, she was the only family Elvis had had. It was the only home he had ever known. The idea occurred to Jesse like it never had before. All of a sudden Elvis looked different to him. He looked more delicate, more fragile. More needful.

It was a home Elvis needed, Jesse realized. A family.

And Jesse was the only family he had.

"We've got a problem," said Randolph the next morning. Jesse, Elvis, Glen, and Annie were on their way to the cove when they met Randolph and Nadine along the trail.

They followed Randolph to the cove and saw immediately that he had been right. Luna was washed up onto the beach again, her nose up on the rocks. A group of Coastal Marine Patrol personnel and veterinarians had already joined together and was trying to roll her back into the water. Jesse and the others immediately began to help. Then Randolph pulled Jesse aside and took him to his pickup truck.

"Where are we going?" asked Jesse.

"Luna's not better," said Randolph. "We have to try something else."

"What?"

"I'll explain as we go."

Just then Elvis ran up beside them. "I'm going, too!" he said, eager to help.

"Stay here, Elvis," said Randolph.

"But I can help," insisted Elvis.

Jesse turned to Elvis. "No," he said with finality. "This is between Randolph and me."

Then Jesse and Randolph climbed into the truck and drove away.

Elvis turned back to the water. By now the team of people trying to get Luna back into the water had completely surrounded the whale. Elvis tried to help, squeezing between the others and trying to get his hands on Luna.

Then he felt someone touch his shoulder and pull him away. It was Glen.

"Stand back, Elvis," said Glen.

"Glen, I can help," said Elvis. "I could . . ."

"Not now," said Glen.

Undaunted, Elvis eagerly squeezed next to Annie.

"I want to help," he told her.

"Elvis!" yelled Annie, fearful the small boy might be trampled by all the people surrounding Luna. "It's dangerous," she said, pulling him away. "Please, just go back to the beach."

Elvis didn't get it. At first everyone complained when he wouldn't pitch in and help pack for the vacation or set up the tent. Now, it seemed, nobody wanted him to help at all!

Upset, he ran into the woods and back to the campsite. He was angry. He felt left out. He decided he didn't need a family. He didn't need a home. If nobody wanted him, that was fine with him. He was sure he could make it on his own.

All he needed was some money to get him started. So he slipped into Glen and Annie's tent and rummaged through their belongings until he found Glen's wallet. He opened the wallet to make sure it had what he needed. He wasn't disappointed. In addition to cash there were lots of credit cards.

He stuffed the wallet into his belt and ran away from the campsite and toward the village. Soon, he thought, he would be away from the Greenwoods and Jesse and the whales and all their problems.

He would be on his own — and free.

Chapter 22

When Glen and Annie had finished helping the others get Luna back into the water they both looked about the beach for Elvis, but he was nowhere to be seen.

"Where is he?" Glen asked Annie.

"I told him to stay up on the beach, out of the way," said Annie. "I didn't want him to get hurt." Suddenly Annie stopped short. She had remembered her earlier promise to Elvis, that he would be able to pitch in and help. "Oh, no," she said.

"What?"

"I broke a promise."

"What promise?" asked Glen.

"And I even did a spit-shake on it," added

Annie. Then she took off toward the campsite.

"You did a spit-shake with somebody?" asked Glen with a grin. "That's pretty serious." And he took off after her.

A few minutes later they reached the campsite. They searched all around, but Elvis wasn't there. Searching his own tent, Glen realized that his wallet was missing. He and Annie concluded that Elvis must have taken Glen's wallet and run away.

"Elvis has left the building," Glen said, his voice wry. "And he took my wallet with him."

"We have to go look for him," said Annie.

"I've got a better idea," Glen said angrily. "Why don't you go look for him?"

Annie was taken aback. "What are you saying?"

"I'm saying I'm tired of this garbage that kid has been putting us through," Glen admitted, looking away from Annie.

"His feelings are hurt," Annie shot back. "He needs us. He just needs someone to give him a break."

"But why do we have to do it?" asked Glen. There was a pleading quality in his voice. "Why do we have to rehabilitate every troubled kid who comes within a mile of us?"

"Tell me you weren't trouble when you were his age."

Glen paused, thinking back to the rough times he had when he was a kid. "Yeah, I was trouble," he admitted. "And this is my punishment."

Annie moved close to Glen and tenderly wrapped her arms around his waist. "Tell me you didn't need someone to love you," she said.

"That's why I have you," said Glen, fighting back the urge to blush.

"But what about Elvis?" Annie asked. "Who does he have?"

Glen looked at Annie. He knew, as usual, that she was right. Together they left the campsite and headed for the police.

"There are other medicines besides the ones Dr. Haley believes in," Randolph told Jesse as he guided the pickup truck around a bend in the coastal road and brought it to a stop. Then he got out and led Jesse through the woods to a flat area at the base of a waterfall. "All medicine comes from the same place, from our mother the earth."

Randolph kneeled down on the bank of a small spring and began digging out what looked to Jesse to be some weeds that were growing there. At first Jesse thought that Randolph was just clearing the bank of the weeds, but Randolph had taken out a spade and was digging deep into the ground. He dug the weeds out roots and all.

Next Randolph washed the plants in the still spring water. Then taking a small bowl and crusher out from a pouch, he put the plants in the bowl and ground them into a paste.

"What is that?" Jesse asked.

"I am grinding these herbs into Skookum," explained Randolph. "It's very strong."

"How strong?"

Randolph took Jesse's hand and pressed his finger into the bowl. Then Jesse brought his finger to his lips and tasted the paste.

"I can taste it!" he exclaimed. "That's pretty strong."

"When we're done with this," began

Randolph, "it'll be even stronger. Our medicine is one that you have to be sick to use. If you're not sick, it's so strong it will kill you."

When he was finished preparing the medicine, he put it in his pouch. Then he and Jesse drove back to the cove. By the time they got there the sun had set. They climbed onto the swim platform that Jesse had used the day before. Luna was in the water next to the platform.

Willy came over and lolled near Jesse. Meanwhile, Littlespot was circling just a few yards away.

Jesse looked into Willy's eyes. This time there was no tension between them. Jesse realized that the whale had begun to trust him again.

At Randolph's request Jesse gave Willy the signal to open his mouth. As soon as Willy did this Luna did the same thing.

That was what Randolph wanted. He took the Skookum out of his pouch and carefully began to apply some to Luna's tongue.

Jesse watched. Something was happening to Randolph. His eyes were now closed and his breathing had become more rhythmic, more musical. Then he began to chant a melody in Haida.

Jesse didn't understand the words to the song. Then he looked at Willy. Willy was watching Randolph. Did Willy understand the song? Jesse wondered.

"It's going to be okay," Jesse said stroking Willy. "She's going to be okay. It's going to work."

Suddenly Randolph stopped singing.

Then Jesse noticed that a tear seemed to be falling from Willy's eye.

"Randolph?" asked Jesse.

"Yes, Jesse?"

"Can a whale cry?"

Randolph glanced at Willy. The whale was already covered with droplets of water. One may have streamed down across his eyes.

"It's probably seawater, Jesse," said Randolph.

"Yeah," Jesse reluctantly agreed. "Probably." But by then a tear was falling out of his own eye, as well.

After the ceremony was over, Jesse and Randolph walked up the dock.

"We've done everything in our power, Jesse," said Randolph as he removed his pouch from his shoulder and threw it into his pickup truck. "All we can do now is let them sleep on it."

"Wait and see if the spirits are with us?" asked Jesse.

"The spirits are always with us," explained Randolph. "It's luck that we need to be with us tonight."

Chapter 23

The next morning a crowd had formed at the cove. Word had spread quickly that Luna was looking better. By the time Dr. Haley joined Randolph on the pier, Willy and Littlespot were circling in the water. Now Luna was circling with them.

"Looks like Luna's getting better," Dr. Haley said, smiling. She was glad all the effort it took to give Luna the antibiotic was paying off.

"Yep," agreed Randolph, thinking of the night before and all the effort it took to administer the Skookum. "My medicine is very powerful."

"*Your* medicine?" Dr. Haley asked quizzically.

Randolph hesitated. "Did I say that?" he asked. "I mean, *your* medicine."

For a moment they both watched as Luna frolicked with her brothers. Haley was a scientist, but she knew that a living creature's recovery can sometimes depend less on medicine than on faith.

"Whatever you did," she finally told Randolph. "I'm glad you did it."

Randolph smiled proudly.

Dr. Haley wasn't smiling as she rejoined Commander Blake a few minutes later. The two stood at the shore end of the pier while Dr. Haley's assistants began preparing the outboard motorboat to take her out to the whales. Getting Luna healthy was only part of the problem, Dr. Haley had come to realize. Earlier, Commander Blake had informed her that the oil slick from *The Dakar* would reach the cove within hours. He and his men were going to seal off the cove with a boom, but if the whales were not out of the cove soon there was no way they could avoid swimming right into the oil.

Then there was John Milner. Despite his insistance that his main concern was to save the whales, deep down Dr. Haley knew otherwise. She, like everyone else, knew that his main concern was to save the reputation of Benbrook Oil. Still, they needed to trust each other if both were going to achieve their separate goals. He had come up with a plan to save the whales in the event that she couldn't get them out to sea in time. He had arranged to have the whales airlifted out of the cove and flown to a nearby marine rescue center where, Milner promised, they would be cared for while they recuperated. He said that Benbrook Oil would eat the cost of the recuperation, but she had her doubts.

Dr. Haley knew she had to work fast. She had to get the whales out to sea. It was the only way she could be certain that they would survive. But now, as she climbed into the motorboat, she remembered her first encounter with Willy. She wondered if the whales would respond to her when she tried to direct them away from the cove.

She would need help. When she saw

Jesse approaching the pier, she quickly changed course and steered the motorboat toward him.

"You're coming with me," she told Jesse.

Jesse listened as Dr. Haley described the situation to him. Then he climbed into the motorboat with her and the two of them rode deeper into the cove.

Dr. Haley stopped the boat when she reached Luna. Willy and Littlespot floated nearby, still standing guard around their sister. Dr. Haley nodded to Jesse.

Jesse knew what to do. He stood up in the boat as it lolled from side to side and he signaled to Willy to come to him.

"This is it, Willy," Jesse told the whale. "We've got to get you out of here now. You've got to make Luna leave. Okay?"

Jesse looked into Willy's eyes and could tell that the whale understood. Then he nodded at Dr. Haley. She revved up the engine and began heading away from the cove toward the open sea. Jesse remained standing as the boat took off. He whistled and waved to Willy.

"This way, Willy!" he shouted back. "Come on!"

Willy spouted and began following the

boat. Soon Littlespot followed suit. Finally, Luna began moving with them, but at a much slower speed. Suddenly she dove beneath the water.

"She hasn't had enough time to recuperate," Dr. Haley said, exchanging a concerned glance with Jesse.

Then Luna reappeared.

"Let's go, Luna!" Jesse shouted encouragingly.

"Just a little farther and we're home free," said Dr. Haley as she drove the boat out of the cove.

Just then Jesse noticed that all three whales had dived beneath the water. And this time they weren't resurfacing. He signaled to Dr. Haley, who cut the engine. The boat came to a stop.

"Where are they?" Jesse wondered aloud.

"Maybe they're past us," said Dr. Haley. "Underwater. Heading out to sea."

Then Jesse looked back toward the cove. His heart sank. The whales had returned to the starting point and had gone back to swimming in circles around the cove. Of the three, Luna looked the most worn out.

It had been too much for her.

Jesse and Dr. Haley returned to the pier, both looking dour and defeated. By now the Coastal Marine Patrol boats were moving in and sealing off the cove with boom nets.

Nadine and Randolph were waiting on the pier as Jesse and Dr. Haley climbed out of the boat.

"They've given the order to boom off the cove," said Randolph. "Seal it completely to keep out the oil, protect the whales."

"Protect them?" asked Jesse angrily. "Don't you mean *trap* them?"

"The nets are for the whale's protection, Jesse," Dr. Haley tried to explain. "An hour from now, if they swam out of the cove, they'd be swimming right into the oil. They'd die."

"If they're trapped in the cove they'll never get back to J-pod!" exclaimed Jesse. "Their family!"

"You saw what happened, Jesse," said Dr. Haley. "The whales won't leave. Luna is not ready. It's for their own good."

"No, it's not!" insisted Jesse. "Not hurting them in the first place would have been for their own good! Not ruining their home would have been for their own good!" Then he stormed off down the pier.

Dr. Haley looked at Randolph. Earlier she had told him of Milner's plan to move the whales to the marine rescue center. Now she and Randolph were thinking the same thing. If Jesse felt this strongly about giving up trying to get the whales back out to sea, how was he going to react when he learned what was planned for them next?

Chapter 24

Elvis had tried his best to get back to the mainland, but there were no ferries leaving until morning. He assumed that Glen and Annie had become worried and probably called the police as soon as they discovered him missing. How soon before he was caught? he wondered. He needed a place to spend the night where he wouldn't be seen. Luckily, he noticed that many of the boats that were docked along the harbor were covered with canvas tarps. He climbed into one and fell asleep there, hidden from view.

When he awoke the next morning, he felt

hungry. He also felt scared. He remembered New York, when his mother was alive. He had felt hungry in the mornings there, too. Often his mother would go out the night before and not return until late the next day. In the beginning Elvis had been too young to know how to make his own breakfast. But even as he got older there would sometimes be no food in the apartment for him to eat. And there would be no money, either.

Then Elvis remembered that he had Glen's wallet in his belt. He pulled it out and opened it. There were a couple of hundred dollars there, money Glen must have taken for the trip. Elvis smiled. It was more money than he had ever seen. He knew he could eat for months on it.

He climbed out of the boat and walked down the dock until he found a donut shop. The case was filled with all different kinds of donuts. Elvis felt as if he could eat them all.

"What can I get you?" the counter clerk asked him.

"Gimme a jelly-filled and a coffee, black," replied Elvis.

Elvis took his donut, paid for it, and slid into a booth. He was just about to take a bite of the donut when he heard a voice coming from the booth next to his.

"We haven't taken an orca out of the wild in over twenty years and now there're three right in my hands," said the voice. Mention of the word "orca" made Elvis listen closely. "Million dollars for each of the young ones," the voice continued, "and two mill for the older brother. The two males are particularly attractive because of their breeding capabilities. But the older brother is already trained. He's a gold mine."

"Listen, Wilcox," came a second voice. Elvis recognized it instantly. It was John Milner's! "You have to be very careful. I told the press these whales were going in for rehab."

"Don't worry, you're covered," replied Wilcox. "These whales are seriously sick and they need our expertise. Long-term rehabilitation is what they need."

"Just so long as it looks like we have the whales' best interests at heart," said Milner. "That's all that matters to me."

"That and your ten percent," said Wilcox. "Besides, we *do* have their interests at heart. They'll be well cared for, I promise you. And in the meantime, while they're getting nice and healthy, there's no reason people shouldn't pay to see them, right?"

Elvis suddenly realized that the whales the two men were talking about were Willy, Luna, and Littlespot. He became alarmed. If the whales were taken away, how would they be reunited with their mother? He wondered: Did Jesse know of this plan?

He decided that something was terribly wrong. Then he slipped carefully out of his seat. When he was certain that Milner couldn't see him, he left the restaurant.

It took only a few minutes for Elvis to hitchhike a ride to the campsite. Along the way the driver turned on the radio just as a startling report was being broadcast.

"Authorities are now saying," announced the voice on the radio, "that fuel vapors ignited, causing an explosion which was heard miles away and igniting the oil slick itself. All island residents are being asked to evacuate at this time."

Elvis suspected immediately that the reporter was talking about *The Dakar*. His suspicions were confirmed when the car he was in pulled over a winding hill that gave him an unobstructed view of the cove. The oil slick had caught fire. And the fire was heading slowly toward Willy, Littlespot, and Luna!

Chapter 25

The car came to a stop at the outer edge of the campsite and Elvis jumped out, slamming the door. Before he could reach the campsite, Jesse and Nadine were upon him.

"Where the heck have you been?" Jesse demanded. "Glen and Annie have been out all night looking for you!"

"I've been out saving your blubbery butt," replied Elvis sharply.

"What are you talking about?"

"I'll tell you, but you have to trust me."

Jesse looked at Elvis suspiciously. "Why should I trust you?"

"Because nobody ever has," Elvis replied.

Then Elvis told Jesse and Nadine all about how he overheard Milner in the donut shop planning to take the whales away. Jesse and Nadine looked at each other. This time they knew that Elvis was telling the truth. Without saying another word the three kids took off for the cove.

By the time they arrived there were several boats in the cove. The people in the boats were attempting to herd the whales with long prongs. In one of the boats a huge crane carried a net that was being directed toward Littlespot.

Some people were on the pier watching. Dr. Haley and Randolph were there. And Milner was there, too. He had a pleased expression on his face.

Jesse ran straight up to Milner and pulled him around by the arm.

"You're a liar!" he shouted accusingly at Milner. "You're not trying to help these whales! You're selling them to an aquarium!"

Dr. Haley took a step toward Jesse. "Jesse," she began. "I assure you they'll be returned to their natural habitat as soon as they're ready."

"Not if *he* has anything to do with it!" Elvis said, pointing to the man in the fishing boat with the crane. It was Wilcox, the same man he saw Milner talking to in the donut shop.

"You're going to lock 'em up, throw away the key!" Jesse shouted at Milner.

Milner was unmoved by Jesse's accusations. "I'm afraid you're going to have to leave, kids," he said coldly. Then he motioned for a security guard. The guard came over and began leading the kids away.

"You're not going to get away with this!" Jesse shouted at Milner as he reluctantly moved away from the pier. He now saw that Willy's brother had been caught in the net.

Jesse broke away from the others and ran toward Milner. "You promised!" he screamed. Then he shoved the business-suited executive hard. Milner stumbled, then lost his balance, and fell backwards off the dock and into the water.

Just then some of the people standing on the pier began calling warnings out to the fishing boat. Jesse looked up. Willy dove underneath the boat with the crane and was now trying to flip it over with his powerful tail. The boat heaved up and went flying into the air. Wilcox and the other passengers toppled out into the water. Then the boat came crashing down beside them.

The net that had been attached to the crane fell loose and Littlespot broke free.

Jesse wanted to jump up and down and cheer, but he knew there was no time. Willy had made the first move by rescuing Littlespot. Now Jesse had to act quickly if he was going to save Willy.

A plan began forming in his head. He wasn't sure it would work, but he had to try something. He ran back to the shore end of the pier and whispered some instructions to Elvis. Elvis gave Jesse a thumbs-up and then headed for a section of the dock where some more of Wilcox's fishing boats were waiting.

Elvis was too little and wiry to be noticed by any of Wilcox's men. Following Jesse's instructions he moved from boat to boat and quietly began tying their anchor ropes directly to the beams of the dock.

Meanwhile, Jesse ran to the other end

of the dock until he reached *The Little Dipper*, the boat he and the Greenwoods had brought from home. Nadine caught up with him just as he jumped on board.

"What are you doing?" she asked breathlessly.

"Hop in," said Jesse as he untied the boat from the dock.

Nadine hesitated. "You know how to drive this thing by yourself?"

"Don't worry about it," said Jesse, remembering the instructions Glen had given him while the boat had been docked in their driveway back home. "Hurry!"

Nadine jumped onto the deck of the ship just as Jesse kicked in the ignition and backed the boat away from the dock.

Jesse guided the boat toward the end of the dock until he reached the swim platform. Elvis was waiting there for him, just as Jesse had instructed.

"All set?" Jesse asked Elvis.

Elvis nodded enthusiastically. "Let's get out of here!" he exclaimed as he hopped on to *The Little Dipper*. Then Jesse revved the motor of the boat again and began driving toward the boom that the Coastal Marine Patrol had laid down to separate the cove from the open sea.

When they were a few yards away from the boom, Jesse cut the motor and brought the boat to a stop.

"Willy!" he called out. "Willy!"

A second later the water surface broke and Willy, Littlespot, and Luna emerged. They swam up alongside *The Little Dipper* and spouted.

"We're getting out of here," Jesse said to Willy. "Okay? Here's one for the old days."

Jesse looked into Willy's eyes. There was an excited gleam in them as if the great whale understood everything that Jesse said.

Then Jesse lifted his hand in a familiar signal. "Remember?" he asked. "They want a captive whale! Let's give 'em a show!"

At that Willy dove under the water and disappeared. Then Jesse started the boat up again and continued toward the boom. The closer he got to it the faster he went.

By now everyone on the pier was watching Jesse and wondering what he was up to. Dr. Haley watched pensively. But when she looked over at Randolph she saw he had a wide smile on his face.

He knew exactly what Jesse had in mind and was sorry he hadn't thought of it himself.

Jesse guided the boat closer to the boom. The boat was almost close enough to touch the boom when Jesse suddenly veered away. As soon as he did this the water parted. Willy exploded through the surface, straight up into the air, from head to tail. The great whale rose higher and higher, like a rocket blasting off into the sky. For a moment it even seemed as if Willy hovered in midair, frozen as if in a photograph.

Then he came down and crashed his full weight onto the nets of the boom until they collapsed beneath his massive form. The boom snapped apart and now there was a hole that led straight out toward the open sea.

Coming up close behind Willy, Littlespot was gently guiding Luna toward the open hole. Willy then emerged from the water and joined in. He and his brother began to pick up speed as they pushed her, jump-starting her toward the hole.

Jesse turned the boat back toward the hole and steered through it.

"Jesse, look!" shouted Nadine. "They're coming after us!"

Jesse and Elvis looked back toward the dock. Wilcox had been fished out of the water and was now leading his team toward his other boats at the dock.

Elvis raised his eyebrow and smiled. "Guess again," he told Nadine.

The kids watched as Wilcox and his men climbed into a boat and revved it up. But no sooner had they started it away from the pier than its line pulled taut and the boat stopped dead in its tracks, sending Wilcox and the others flying into the water.

The kids laughed. Jesse's plan had worked!

But their joy was short-lived. All of a sudden a great wave of heat mixed in with the cool winds of the sea. The air around them became thick with clouds of black smoke. Just a few feet ahead of them was the oil slick. And it was still on fire.

Jesse knew that Willy and the other whales were underwater, trying to head out to sea, but by now had probably stopped because of the oil. He had to figure out a way to help them get around the slick, but now *The Little Dipper* was enveloped in smoke.

Jesse couldn't see a thing.

Chapter 26

Glen and Annie had seen everything from a rock that overlooked the cove. Tired and disheveled, they had just come back from their unsuccessful search for Elvis when they saw *The Little Dipper* racing around the cove heading for the boom.

By the time they reached the cove, *The Little Dipper* was already engulfed in smoke from the oil slick fire. They sensed immediately that Jesse was on the boat. Both were in a near-panic when Randolph waved them over and led them to his ship, *The Natselane*.

While he was getting *The Natselane* ready to go, Randolph explained everything to the Greenwoods. How Jesse had taken *The Little Dipper*. How he and Willy broke through the boom. How Willy and Littlespot guided Luna toward the open sea.

But now there was real danger. Not only were the whales probably trapped below the water, but Jesse, Nadine, and Elvis were trapped inside the smoke from the fire.

As soon as they were underway and heading toward *The Little Dipper*, Randolph radioed the Coastal Marine Patrol for help.

"Mayday. Mayday," he said. "This is *The Natselane*. We're at Turner Point. There's a small pleasure craft trapped in the fire!"

Annie and Glen looked at each other. They were scared. Really scared. Each prayed they would reach the kids in time.

Chapter 27

"Jesse, I'm scared," cried Nadine as she held on to Jesse's arm. Her face was covered with black soot and she was having trouble breathing.

"Me, too," was all that Jesse could say. Although his hands were on the wheel of the boat he had no idea which way to turn it. If he steered the boat the wrong way they might drive right into the center of the fire.

Just then Elvis caught sight of something ahead.

"Hey, you guys," he called out. "I see something in the water. Something big."

"What, like fish?" asked Nadine, hoping it might be the whales.

"No," said Elvis. "More like rocks."

Just then *The Little Dipper* crashed into a snag of jagged rocks that tore through its hull. The kids were thrown to the deck as water began pouring into the hull of the ship.

Then the boat lunged to one side and began to sink!

Elvis grabbed Jesse by the collar. He was in a panic. "If you get me out of this," he yelled, "I'll never touch your stuff or cross the line or say bad things about you ever again!"

For a moment Jesse forgot about the immediate danger they were in. "Promise?" he asked. Elvis nodded. But then a gush of water exploded over the side of the ship. Jesse grabbed Elvis tightly making sure he wouldn't drown. "I'm not going to ever let anything happen to you!" he promised.

Just then the sound of a motor cut through the noise around them. The kids looked up and saw a Coastal Marine Patrol helicopter descending toward them through the smoke.

"Hey!" Nadine called upward. "We're down here!"

A rescue officer leaned out of the helicopter and lowered a harness attached to a cable. Jesse raised his arms, water rising around his knees, and eagerly awaited the harness. But when he got hold of it, his heart sank. They would have to go up one at a time.

"Jesse — " started Nadine as she realized the same thing.

"I know!" exclaimed Jesse. "There's only room for one!"

"You go!" said Nadine.

"No!" Jesse said with finality. "You go!"

Then Jesse helped Elvis, lifting him into the harness. For a short moment they looked into each other's eyes without saying a word. Tears began to fall from Elvis's eyes.

"You're the best brother I ever had!" Elvis finally let out. Then he hugged Jesse tightly.

"I'm the *only* brother you ever had," replied Jesse. Then he broke the hug. Time was running out. He motioned up to the helicopter and the harness began to ascend away from the sinking boat.

"I'm scared!" Elvis shouted as the harness lifted.

"Don't worry, kid!" Jesse shouted back. "It's just like bungee jumping!"

"I never went bungee jumping! I lied," admitted Elvis tearfully. *I lied!*

But by then Elvis was too far away for Jesse to hear. The rescue harness had disappeared into the clouds of black smoke. Now all he could think about was the water that was rising around his thighs.

When the empty harness returned, Jesse helped Nadine put it on, then watched her be swallowed up by the black smoke, too.

"Come on, come on," he muttered impatiently to himself as he struggled to see the helicopter through the plumes of smoke. Jesse wondered how long it would take the rescue officer to send the harness down a third time. *The Little Dipper* seemed to be sinking faster. He was holding on to the railing around the helm, but the water had risen up around his waist.

Finally, the empty harness reappeared through the darkness. Jesse reached up and grabbed its sides.

"Go!" Jesse shouted up to the helicopter.

"Secure yourself!" he heard one of the rescue officers shout back.

"I'm on!" replied Jesse. "Go! Go!"

Jesse was still trying to climb into the harness as it began to rise into the sky. His legs dangled in the air and he felt himself being pulled in great swings as the helicopter above began flying through the smoke.

But Jesse felt something was wrong. Try as he might he couldn't keep a firm grip on the harness. His hands, oily from the water and the soot of the fire, kept sliding off. Finally he lost his grip completely and plummeted back toward the sea and straight into the ring of fire!

Chapter 28

Jesse fell through the ring of fire and into the water. He felt himself sinking uncontrollably into the depths. Finally, he began to slow down. Holding his breath he fought his way back up until he broke through the oily surface. All around him were flames and clouds of smoke.

"Help!" he cried, spitting and swallowing water at the same time. The air was too thick to breathe. "Help!"

Jesse knew he wouldn't be able to hold on much longer. He could hardly breathe, his legs were too weak to tread water, and his head was becoming dizzy. If somebody didn't find him soon, he realized, he might not make it out alive.

Soon Jesse's arms became too tired to hold him above water and he began to sink. Oily water bubbled into his mouth. He coughed up some of the black substance and knew that some of the oil had entered his lungs. He knew then that only a miracle could save him.

That's when he saw something moving toward him from the distance. Something was pushing through the water. Something big. *A ship*, Jesse thought. *Someone must have sent a ship*. But as the form approached him he realized that it wasn't a ship at all.

All of a sudden the big thing raised itself further out of the water and a huge black eye blinked at Jesse. It was Willy, Jesse realized in amazement. Willy!

Willy floated alongside Jesse until Jesse was able to grab hold of his bent dorsal fin. Then he sank, taking Jesse with him, below the water.

After a few seconds Willy broke the surface again. Jesse was holding on to his dorsal fin, riding his back. All around them were walls of fire. There seemed to be no escape.

Willy floated there for a moment, hesitating. Jesse knew why. The only way to get through the ring of fire was to go under it. Was Willy waiting for his signal, he wondered?

"Go for it, Willy," he told the whale. "Go for it."

Jesse took a deep breath, holding Willy's fin with one hand and his own nose with the other. Then Willy angled down and dove into the water. Down they went, deep below the surface. Then Willy leveled out and began heading straight. Above him Jesse could see the strange colors made by the ring of fire recede into the distance. But now he was beginning to run out of breath. Just then Willy angled upward again and began rising. Jesse wasn't sure how much longer he could hold on.

Finally they broke through the water and into the atmosphere. Jesse let go of his nose and began gasping for air. Here the air was cool again. He glanced back and saw that the ring of fire was now behind them. They had gotten through!

"Jesse!" he heard someone calling to him. "Jesse!"

Jesse looked in the other direction. It was Annie. And she was calling to him from *The Natselane*. Before long the boat pulled up alongside him. Randolph and Glen reached over the side and pulled him on board as Annie ran up and wrapped her arms around him, hugging him tightly.

Willy lolled alongside the ship.

"You saved his life, Willy," Annie leaned over and said to the orca.

"Thanks, Willy," Jesse added happily.

Willy shot a plume of water from his spout. He seemed happy, too.

Chapter 29

A few minutes later the Coastal Marine Patrol boat arrived, putting Elvis and Nadine on to the deck of *The Natselane*. Annie, Glen, and Jesse helped them out. Nadine and Jesse hugged for a long moment. Up until then neither had been certain if they would see each other again.

Annie hugged Elvis while Glen tousled his hair.

"You don't have to say it," Elvis said to them. "I shouldn't have run away. I'm sorry."

"I'm sorry I broke my promise," said Annie, not bothering to fight back her tears. "It'll never happen again."

Randolph steered the boat away from the fire and started it back toward the cove. Just then he saw something rise up in front of the ship.

"Willy," he said in recognition.

Jesse climbed down to the lower deck and leaned over the railing. He got as close as he could to Willy.

"You did it, boy," he told the whale.

But Willy still didn't move away from Jesse.

"Go on," Jesse said. "You have to go. Be a family again."

Willy let out a sad cry. Jesse's eyes welled up with tears.

"I don't want you to go, either," said Jesse. "But you have to. You have the best thing anybody could ever have. You have your family. You have your mom."

Willy cried again.

"He won't leave," said Glen.

"What's he waiting for?" asked Jesse.

Randolph had cut the engine and joined them on deck. "Jesse, he's waiting for you to give the signal."

Jesse knew what Randolph meant. He nodded and then braced himself. As soon as he gave the signal, he knew he might never see Willy again.

"I love you, Willy," he said to the whale. Then he pulled his arm back and thrust it forward.

Willy understood the signal and slowly turned away from the ship. Then he dropped beneath the water. A few seconds later he reappeared, this time next to Catspaw and the rest of J-pod, and followed them as they swam farther and farther out to sea.

Suddenly each of the whales in the pod began to chatter happily. Soon some of the whales were rubbing up against each other. Others were spyhopping. Finally, the whales began to breach the water, one by one. It looked to Jesse as if they were dancing their way out to sea.

Jesse's tears stopped. His sad, frowning lips turned upward into a happy smile. Willy was where he belonged now, he thought to himself. And that was how it should be.

After a few moments Randolph started up the engine of *The Natselane* and began steering the ship toward the shore.

Nadine walked over to Jesse and saw that his eyes were straining to look out at the open sea, searching for any remaining sign of Willy.

But by now the whales had long vanished from view.

"You could come back next summer," Nadine told him. "When J-pod returns."

Jesse shot a glance at Nadine. "Couldn't we do something before that?"

Nadine blushed. "You mean, without Willy?"

"Yeah," smiled Jesse. That was exactly what he meant. Then Jesse looked past Nadine at Elvis, who was staring right at them. "What are you looking at?" he demanded.

"What are *you* looking at?" Elvis snapped back defiantly. Then he reached into his pocket and handed something to Jesse. "This is for you."

"What is it?"

"It's why I hated your guts."

Jesse looked down. It was a picture.

"Mom," said Jesse as he recognized the person in the snapshot. And next to her was Jesse, when he was much, much younger. Only the picture was taped together down the center as if someone had ripped Jesse out of it and then put him back later.

"The only picture of her I ever had," said Elvis, "and you had to be in it. It kind of had an accident. But I taped it back together."

"Thanks," said Jesse. He looked at Elvis. There was something different about his brother now. Something nicer.

"And one more thing," Elvis added. "Our mom. She talked about you all the time. She never stopped talking about you. She really missed you. She felt bad about what happened. She loved you."

Jesse was stunned. He had always hoped to know how his mother had felt about him. Now he knew. He stepped forward and hugged his brother.

"What do you think?" Annie asked Glen loud enough so that Jesse and Elvis could hear.

"I guess we can keep him," Glen said just as loud. "I mean, I would hate to break up the set." Jesse and Elvis stepped apart. "So what do you say, Elvis?" Glen asked.

"You want to stay with us? Be a part of the family?"

"Can I get back to you on that?" Elvis replied jokingly, and then he smiled at all of them. He was home, all right. Home for good.